SALTBROOK: AN ALICIA LAKE INVESTIGATION

Part of the Ravenswood
Institute Files

Dee Arbacauskas

Tormented Artifacts/Dee Arbacauskas

Contents

Acknowledgements

I really didn't think this would happen. You go from making a tarot deck to starting a book for the deck, then locking it away in the back of your head for a decade with a few other things, only to find when you'd unpacked it later that it had eaten itself and somehow grown into a full novel. And then when you get that one written you find out there's a whole universe of other stories and novels right behind it, just waiting to pop out. This is the first one of those.

I'd like to thank my amazing partners for putting up with me as I fumed and swore through every stage of theis process, the editors, proofers, and friends who helped put this whole thing together and who also helped form the backbone of the Thirteenth Chamber community, all of my patrons over on the Tormented Artifacts Patreon page, and also the large stack of [REJECTED: UNREAD BY PUBLISHER/AGENT] notices that convinced me self-publishing this was probably the only way I'd ever even get eyes on these pages.

And lastly, there's every last one of you who willingly grabbed a copy of this book to peruse.

So, to all of you now reading this? Thanks. And welcome to the first entry in the modern era of the Ravenswood Institute.

Prologue

April 14th 19--
Northeastern Washington
2pm

The lake was quiet. Just a small, cool body of water
nestled between ridges too steep and craggy to
be called hills, yet too squat to properly earn the
name mountains, surrounded by thick clusters
of forest. Old pines swayed slightly in the early
spring breeze. The lake was safely tucked back
far and remote enough inside forest preserves to
be almost inaccessible— a single dirt road that
wound and stretched back for miles from the main
highways was the only thing connecting it back to
civilization, leaving it a place few ever visited by
intent, or even by accident.

And so it was today— the waters smooth as
glass and undisturbed, heavy with spring floods,
stretched clear into the trees on all sides, broken
only in one spot near the dead center, where a
single spire of wrought iron thrust up a good ten
feet above the water, the rusted-away welds on
both sides of it where the arms of a cross had been
added onto it and then fallen off again visible to any

boater that got close enough.

And then, with a great boom that could be felt more than heard by anyone standing on the shores of that lake (had there been anyone), that peace was broken. Birds exploded from the trees on all sides, turning and wheeling through the sky in their startlement. Great ripples surged through the water from the south end of the lake clear up to the north and bouncing back again, giving the surface the momentary impression of a storm-tossed sea, and just like that, the waters began to recede. So slowly at first, it seemed almost imperceptible, but then faster and faster, the lake level sinking downwards to reveal first those trees covered in the spring floods, and then as the sides sloped more sharply downwards, trees far older than that— the tips of black waterlogged bare-branched skeletons that had not directly felt the sun in over sixty years emerged. For the next hour, the water continued to drain away.

And in the center of the lake, foot after foot of that spire became exposed to the air, until you could see where it joined to stone at the top of a tower that began to emerge as well from the waters. And the peaked tiled roofs of other buildings surrounding it as well, whole buildings, some still standing intact, others broken from the currents and floods when the lake was first filled. Deposits of mud and sediment swirled up the sides of some buildings like a child's finger paints. Brown in some places, glittering greens and purples in others where heavier metals and other substances had been stirred up. The cold lake waters pulled back slowly, as if they were hesitant to let go of what they had held onto for decades, but finally, after another hour of draining, the streets and paths of the town were exposed, still dressed by thick mud and lake weed in places, but the waters themselves had given up their icy grip. Even in the center of town, where the old dressed-stone well still stood intact, the waters had finally gone. And the town and the valley stood, slowly drying in the spring sun. Waiting.

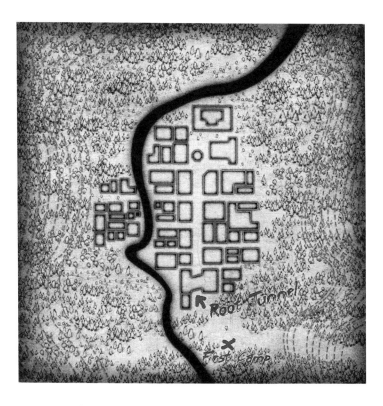

Saltbrook Valley and environs, circa 1910
(modern notations, late summer 2019)

1. Cold Approach

Ice cold water, that's what I remember. The freezing jolt of being submerged so suddenly that your body goes straight past the shock response and directly into full pain, splaying out with every muscle spasming for a moment with the strain, and then just... floating there, in the void. Feeling the water all around me, lungs burning to hold onto what breath I could, eyes shut tight because for some reason I couldn't dare to look, as if looking would somehow make it all the more real. My outstretched hands reached blindly, hoping to find which way was even upwards, and touched metal that was even colder than the water surrounding me, metal so cold it burned and—

I woke up, gasping, the phone next to my head on the car seat ringing away at maximum volume. I sat up and rubbed my eyes, looking out through the Suburban's windows. The sun was just barely beginning to pick up over the horizon. As I reached for my phone, I could see the callback ID— upstate New York. Then again, there's really only one person that'd be calling me this early while I was on the job. I flipped the phone open.

"Lake Services." I could feel my voice crack with the just-woke-up need for water. Then again, I hadn't pulled off the road to take a break until.. how late had it been? How little sleep had I actually gotten? Everything felt muffled, my own thoughts wrapped in grimy cotton as I was still trying to wake up fully.

"Ms. Lake," came the reply. The same cultured lack-of-accent that screamed the upper heavily— moneyed northeast of the United States that I'd had a few calls with now on this case. And yet he insisted on introducing himself again. "Ambrose Hollowell from the Ravenswood Institute. I must apologize for calling so early, I heard your message from last night regarding our mutual quarry, and had an update of my own to share as well." he paused for a moment. "...Are you awake enough for me to continue?"

While he'd been pattering, I'd reached forward to

the cupholder next to the driver's seat, grabbed what remained of a bottle of water, and managed to swig enough down to at least get my throat working all the way. I cleared my throat and then spoke. "Go ahead, Ambrose, it's your dime, after all."

"Excellent. Well, first and foremost, We concur with your opinion— based on the police report it does appear that our Mr. Wallace has indeed broken into the wildlife reserve at Saltbrook Valley and gone to ground there. Our people were finally able to identify the item he took from the Institute Archives, and being that they too came originally to us from Saltbrook, I'd say that double-confirms your findings."

"Great. Then since he's on federal land in a state I'm not even licensed for, I'm assuming you don't need me on the contract anymore?" I slid open the side door of the Suburban and stepped down onto the asphalt of the rest stop I'd finally parked in last night, to begin stretching and limbering up. Even in a vehicle as big as mine, car-sleeping never really felt like rest— every muscle and joint just wanted to start knotting up.

"Quite the contrary, Ms. Lake. We want you on the job in particular. Given your proximity and familiarity with the case already, you're the best option we have. My associates are already working on the legal details that need to be handled to allow you entry into the valley, and I was calling to simply apprise you of that, as well as to inform you that we need to change the details of our contract somewhat."

"...change the contract? Just what did you have in mind?" This wasn't how I wanted to wake up. This wasn't how anyone wanted to wake up. I just wanted to get a nice pat on the head for doing the pursuit work, signed off on what they owed me, take a six-hour nap and—

"First, Ms. Lake, you should know that we've authorized and drafted a new payment for this— two hundred thousand, in addition to the fees and expenses you've already accrued." I nearly dropped the phone. That was nearly four times the fee for my high-end cases for investigations or bounties. "That said, we are, as I said before, changing the terms. Apprehension and recovery of Mr. Wallace may no longer be possible, so it is no longer a requirement. However, recovery of the stolen property is now of absolute importance and is your new primary goal. As I said last night, our discovery of which items were taken— you're looking specifically for a ring of keys— a steel ring, about two inches in diameter, with five keys hanging from it. Four of them relatively standard house-sized keys, made from cast or machined steel, the fifth, significantly larger and older looking, made from cast bronze. All of them must be recovered and brought back here. Wallace likely will not have let them out of his sight."

I nearly fumbled the phone before Hollowell could even finish that first sentence. Two hundred thousand was enough, more than enough— pay off some old debts, finally take the vacation I'd been promising myself for the last I don't know how long... it was too good to be true. Something had to be sketchy about this, and I definitely felt like Hollowell was holding out on me.

"Before I agree to anything," I finally said, "I have some questions." Some. Hah. The problem was more that I still felt barely awake enough to even be thinking through everything. "First off, what is so important about these keys that someone will grab them, drive for almost 48 hours straight cross-country, and take them to the middle of nowhere?"

Hollowell paused before answering. That should have warned me, though I was too tired to pick up on it fully. "The keys have... certain historical value to the Institute, especially the fifth one, given its age and its hand-shaped nature. They might have some value to outside collectors as well, but likely less than what we're offering for them."

"All right, assuming I accept that, then secondly, just HOW is Wallace capable of that fortyeight hour drive— I've been in pursuits, but this is unnatural. No stops to sleep, no food, the only thing he stopped for was more gas. This is the first pursuit case where I've never been able to make up time on a chase because he simply hasn't stopped at all. How is he doing this?"

"Well, without seeing him myself Ms. Lake, I can hardly make any kind of judgment, other than that he has been acting out of character for a while now. We had in fact, recommended and referred him to an associated therapist that he'd been seeing for several months before this, though he did skip his last appointment, which would have been the day before the theft. I'm sure you've had experience with targets in an unstable frame of mind before, and have seen just how unpredictably they might act under certain pressures. That said, he is certainly not the Frank Wallace I hired for the position, and should obviously be treated with a large amount of caution when you do encounter him."

That was about as much of a non-answer as I could expect. "All right. Last question— just how dangerous is this Saltwood area? Why such a high amount of hazard pay?"

"Salt*brook*, not Saltwood, Ms. Lake. As for how dangerous, one can assume fairly lethal, from what little I've read, very few of the people who've entered the refuge since it reopened have survived. As to the specific dangers, you'd need to talk to the rangers on-site for a more accurate picture. Now, do we have an accord?"

"I don't know. I just woke up when you called. Give me some time to think and wake up, damnit. I'll call you back." I hung up the phone and tossed it onto the passenger seat, finished stretching, and grabbed the running shoes I'd kicked off before falling asleep. The rest area was just big enough to have a paved path that wound around it, presumably for people walking pets and children to work off some of the nervous energy of a long car ride, but right now, this early, I had it to myself, so I started a fast walk around it, to loosen up both legs and brain.

Things weren't adding up. I quickened my pace as I came around the quarter-mile loop, moving from a walk into the all-out stride I'd use during a run-down pursuit. I grabbed the hair tie off my wrist and shoved my braids into a ponytail to keep them out of my face. Hollowell was hiding details, I knew that much, but it sounded more like he was doing it because I'd think he was the crazy one, rather than Wallace. And Wallace himself... Schenectady, New York to eastern Washington state in just a little over two days, and the credit card traces I'd ran showed he only stopped for fuel during all that. No meals, no rest, not even a bathroom break. And the one gas station attendant I'd stopped for long enough to question had described him in terms that made him seem more like some kind of meth-addled robot than the "open, jolly, and humorous" description that had been in the file Hollowell had given me.

Another quarter mile. I kicked up the pace into a full jog. I was used to pursuit cases. Even long-term cases. But I was also used to being able to catch up to the target, or to run them down, even if it took time to do it. The fact that Wallace had just kept on gaining time and distance from me the entire chase had thrown me off my game. Still, he was cornered. There was only one way in or out of the refuge according to the police scanner report yesterday, so law enforcement was content to just sit and wait for him to come out. I'd have him to myself to bring down, inside of twenty-five square miles or so of wilderness. And it's not like this was my first time doing wilderness pursuit.

Another quarter mile. Full run now, all out, legs and arms pumping for everything they were worth. What was so dangerous about this place? What made Saltbrook such a risk for the Institute that they couldn't wait for local police to catch him afterwards? Why was the recovery of the keys more important than bringing in Wallace? I didn't have answers, and the only way to get them was to go there and do the job.

One last lap. Pushing past that full run—this wasn't about thought now, this was about endurance, keeping that speed and pushing past everything. My legs and lungs started to burn. Another early riser walking their Shi Tzu caught sight of me coming around a corner and nearly startle-jumped herself off the track. I couldn't help it— my lips skinned back from my teeth in a smile that I'm sure did more to frighten than reassure as I went past. Let's be honest. Any tall rail-thin figure with long braids bouncing behind them like medusa's snakes suddenly appearing on the trail in the predawn shadows would startle someone. Add that I was running all out like I was chasing or being chased by the Devil himself, and well, I would have been startled too. And then, before I knew it, I was rounding that last corner again, slowing down into a lope across the asphalt that took me back to the side of my Suburban.

I didn't have my answers. And every practical sense I had said this was a bad idea. Still, this was almost four times the amount of money I made in a single year. And the only way I was going to get the answers I wanted for this was to do the job. That stubborn sense that made me a decent investigator needed all this to make sense somehow.

I opened up the passenger side door and grabbed my phone, dialing back Hollowell, who answered before even one ring and had finished.

"Ms. Lake?"

"I'll take the job. Email over the new contract, I want this in writing before I get moving from here."

"Excellent, I'll do just that. Once you've signed off on it, proceed to the Saltbrook Refuge. I'll do my best to make sure you're granted entry by the end of the day."

"Thank you. And Hollowell?"

"Yes?"

"No more lies. Or you'll be finding a new investigator when all this is done with." I hung up, climbed into the Suburban, and started to change clothes for the drive.

2. Cautionary Tales

I skipped breakfast, opting to drive straight through the small town of Post Falls. The highway took me further west, across the border into Washington and then Spokane, and then north from there. Four-lane interstates became two-lane highways, and while morning gridlock slowed me at first, both traffic, and any signs of life faded quickly the further north I went. Trees filled my view to both sides of the road, the early fall climate causing the occasional oak or maple in the sea of evergreens to stand out in a breakaway riot of reds and oranges.

The Suburban and I had both worked up an appetite

from driving by the time we reached Colville and the turnoff onto private roads that would take us further north. Like me, my beast of a utility vehicle was more pursuit predator than high-speed ambusher, adept at the long slow chase until the prey fell over from exhaustion. Sadly, though, keeping her fueled was another issue. After eating and gas, what was left of the expense payment from the Institute was looking thin indeed. It was a good thing we were getting to the end of this.

Climbing back in, we drove up further, shifting from Highway 395 to Highway 20, which quickly narrowed down to two lanes of blacktop, the turning off onto private roads, the two lanes turning into gravel, then a single lane of packed dirt, which wound back and forth turning in on itself like some kind of snake as we slowly climbed back up into the foothills. Between all of this, my speed had slowed to a crawl despite the lack of traffic— I wasn't in a huge amount of hurry as I was now on the only road Wallace could use to escape if the thought even occurred to him, and the terrain and hairpin turns would have been suicide at high speed in a Suburban. Another hour of that, and all of it in solid trees and wildlands— not a single turnoff or any signs of habitation through this stretch. No fences, lamps, signs, or anything but the forest to both sides of me, and the trees themselves old growth, grown in so densely that you couldn't even see the roadway moments after it had doubled back on itself. The only hint that anything of modern humanity had been this way was the fact that the road was still here and debris-free.

The road finally emerged from the trees at the highest point of a ridgeline that ran from the southeast to my left, to the northeast to my right, curving to turn almost perfectly from north to south as it went off into the distance. It was a rectangular manmade clearing, sitting on the ridge like a saddle on the back of a horse, roughly the size and shape of a football field. In the middle of the clearing stood a small two-story wood-sided building, most of it built into the solid rock of the ridge, except for the northwestern quarter which hung over the far side into the valley like a watch-station, supported on pilings that sank into the steep face below it. The road continued past the building on that side as well, through a battered metal barricade that had clearly seen a recent impact. Two men stood in front of that barricade, both wearing what looked like forestry service uniforms— brown shirts, pants, and even the hats, one of which was carrying a shotgun of all things. I sighed. This was going to take a bit. Still, I went ahead and let the Suburban slowly roll up to the barricade until the unarmed one raised a hand to stop me.

I went ahead and parked the Suburban where it

sat and swung down out of the driver's seat to begin walking towards the two. The one on the left, a white kid with blonde hair who couldn't have been older than twenty immediately held up the shotgun and trained it on me. He was holding it completely wrong, and firing the thing was more likely to break his arm than hit me, but I wasn't about to point that out right now. I put both hands up.

"That's far enough, lady," he said "this is a federal reserve, and no trespassers are allowed. You need to get back in your car and turn around and—" This was going to get us a whole lot of nowhere unless I took some initiative, so I went ahead and interrupted.

"Look, not to be impolite to someone with a gun on me, but this'll go a lot easier if I can put my hands down and talk, all right? Mind relaxing that a little?" The barrels of the gun didn't waver off of me much, but at least he took his hand away from the trigger. I could work with that. "All right." I continued. "I'm going to reach into my back pocket and pull out a badge, ok?" Blondie said nothing. His companion, who looked more like he'd stepped off the nearby reservation spoke up, coming over my way at the same time.

"You go ahead and do that, ma'am."

"Ma'am? Jesus, do I look that old to you two kids?"

I kept my left hand up and reached for my wallet with my right, unfolding it as I brought it out, so both my driver's license, and more importantly, my PI license right below it were visible. He came in closer, careful to not get in between the firing line between me and Blondie, and took the wallet from my hand.

"Alicia Lake, Private Investigator." He read off from the card.

"And you'll find my bounty hunter card and registration underneath that." I supplied.

"These are for New York."

"And the ones for Pennsylvania and New Jersey are under those first two."

"That's nice and all, but we're a little bit west of that."

"Only a little? Look, the man I've been hired to track down managed to jump a few states, and if what I heard on the scanner was right, he was the same one that came through here yesterday, and crashed through your barricade there. And he's still down in that valley. Now I did check, I do have extradition rights on my side to take him out of here."

"Which is great and all, but you're not authorized to go down in that valley." he replied, handing me back my wallet.

"No, but my employer's supposed to be working on that part of things, and said he'd have something ready by the end of the day today. It's only three o' clock now. I'm perfectly content to wait right here. If he does send something through, we can all move along, and if he doesn't by say, five pm, I'll turn around, go back down, find a hotel, and figure out what's going on from there. That sound all right to you two?"

The man standing next to me turned back to Blondie. "Ok, Charlie, go put that thing back inside."

"But—"

"You really feel up to holding a gun on someone for two hours? Because I don't. We're taking her at her word." He turned back to me. "Sorry, we've both been freaked the fuck out since this whole thing started." He offered a hand to shake. "Call me Cas. That's Charlie." He motioned to Blondie, who was already unloading the shotgun while walking across the open ground to the station.

I took his hand firmly in mine. He had a decent handshake— firm, but no attempt to overpower my own grip. "Alicia, but, you knew that already. Mind if I come inside, stretch my legs a little?" He gave a welcoming gesture towards the building, and I followed him in. "I'd also like to ask about just how things happened last night. This chase has been a bit... weird."

"Well, weird's definitely one way to put it. That barricade's normally just chained shut, and we're just up here on fire watch duty. But around four o'clock yesterday, we saw the dust trails kicking up from the access road, letting us know someone was coming— it's how we saw you today and knew to get outside too. But this— an old white guy pulls up in a rental that looked utterly filthy, and comes right up to the barricade. I came around to one side, tried to get him to roll down his window, but he wouldn't even look at me, just backed the car up to the turn into here, and came straight at the barricade, flooring it the whole time. Front end hit the pole, and it must have wrecked the engine, but he broke on through the barricade, and the car went flying over. There's maybe a quarter-mile of road left on the other side and the car just flipped and slid all the way to the end of that. I yelled for Charlie to grab the medical kit and fire extinguisher, just in case, but by the time we both got done there, he was gone. Driver's side door was hanging open, but he was nowhere in sight. Only place he could've gone was deeper into the valley, but since there's been no formal order to mount a rescue attempt, we weren't going to go any further."

At that point, we were up the steps and inside the building. This had obviously been a house that had been converted out at some later point into something else before getting repurposed as a forestry station. We were standing inside what had to have been a living room space, with an additional dining room around the corner that had a view over the valley below us. In this room, however, was the hub of a small office with more space than it needed— two desks with laptops, phones, fax, and a small radio operator setup. I took in as much detail as I could, but I didn't let it stop me from more questions.

"And why is that? Exactly? I mean, if you're supposed to be keeping people out of the reserve, shouldn't you have gone after him? Or attempted a rescue, since he had to have been injured and was clearly out of his mind?"

"That's what I'm getting to. You don't know about this valley. That said, welcome to what would have been the Saltbrook ruins visitor center."

"Visitor center? Wait. 'Would have been?'"

"This'll be easier if I show you at the same time. Follow me." He led me back into the dining room. While the room did duty as an observation station, with a pair of folding chairs, telescope, and two pairs of binoculars set up by the windows, most of it was taken over by a large table covered with a topographical map of the valley that had likely first been installed in that front room, then moved back here. Wooden sideboards meant to be attached to the walls originally, but were instead stacked leaning against one wall in here bore legends like 'Saltbrook: the town that couldn't' and 'The Coulee Dam Initiative' and finally 'The Saltbrook Tragedy', each with a number of infographics and faded blocks of informative historical text. All of it looked like it had been gathering dust (with the occasional patchy cleaning) for at least a decade.

"I... what?" But Cas had moved past all that to the binoculars— and passed me one set. "This seems a little... much."

"Ok, but look down there. What do you see?"

I reported as I looked with bare eyes "Trees, rocks, what looks like your typical nature preserve."

"Try it with the binoculars." he replied. "Look right out towards the middle there at the treetops."

It took a second to get the binoculars focused on the right area he was indicating, but once I did, it leaped into view— surrounded by treetops, quite a few of which looked to be dead, one stone spire stood just above the height of the treeline, with a single beam of metal sticking straight up from it. Near the top were stubs extending out perpendicular from the main bar of the spire, like... "Wait, is that a steeple?" I tracked downwards with the binoculars and started to see shapes in the random piles of earth, and down at ground level, half buried street signs and other detritus. "Is... that a town?"

"Welcome to what's left of the town of Saltbrook, Washington."

"You realize that just makes more questions than answers, right?"

"Yeah," interrupted Charlie as he came through the living room behind us, "But Cas is our resident nerd for this shit, and he loves winding up the explanations." Cas shot him a look through the open door, but Charlie was already around the corner, headed towards what I presume was the kitchen. He turned back to me, and I put on my best 'done with this' expression and waited.

"OK, so, explaining this is easier if I just do it in full, all right?" I gestured for him to go on. "Saltbrook was founded back in the 1800s as an attempt at a mining and logging town. Named for the small river that runs through the bottom of the valley. Only thing is, the town never really got big."

"Why is that?"

"At first, because too many people took sick and died. They called it Saltbrook because of the taste — the river was leaching off mineral salts as it came down through the mountains into the valley. Problem is, it was also picking up a lot of heavy metals— lead, arsenic, that kind of thing. It took a good five years before they finally got a well sunk into the aquifer under the town that had clean water. Later on, it was because it was so remote. Spokane and other towns were better set up for trade, and this was just too remote to anything for people to want to move up here without some good reason."

"So, no native burial ground hauntings or anything at least." At least he snorted at the joke.

"Fuck no. Tribal records even showed that we, well, the Chualpay and the Wenatchi at least, tried to warn them that the valley was poison, but they didn't want to listen. Anyways, town never really got bigger than five or six hundred people, and then in 1930, they started construction on the Grand Coulee Dam, down on the Columbia. Problem is, a dam that size takes years for the concrete to bear up to the full load, so some of the smaller tributaries like this had to get smaller dams put in to make sure the worst of the load didn't overrun the main dam. The state paid every resident in Saltbrook relocation money to move elsewhere with a three-year deadline, and set things up in two stages to dam off the south end of the valley, with a smaller retaining dam at the north end to hold back the initial flood that'd turn this into a nice tourist lake."

"OK, so, what's the 'Great Saltbrook Tragedy,' then?"

Well, they had three years to move everyone out. Problem is, towards the end of that first year, after the dams were built, there were freak storms. Heaviest rain ever recorded, and it all came down in a matter of hours. When the north retaining dam broke in a landslide that took out the easiest road in or out of the valley, there was almost no warning for anyone. People tried to make it out, but the water flooded in fast enough to cover everything by nightfall. After the count of everyone who made it out, it was estimated that at least eighty-five people got left behind, drowned in the floodwaters."

"And we're back to the mass grave thing. Crap."

"Wait for it. So, the valley spent sixty-plus years underwater. Never took off as a good lake for fishing or even for tourists, because it was too remote and too small. So, after the final rigidity tests on Coulee Dam passed in the nineties, it was deemed safe to go ahead and remove the dam at the south end of this valley, let the tributary flow normally again. So they did, and after a month of letting things drain out and dry out, a team of environmental survey scientists went in — partly to determine if it'd be safe to reopen the valley as part of the park reserve, and partly to see what the effects on flooding and draining the town were, since this isn't the kind of thing that happens every day. Three days later when none of the scientists came back out or had any contact, the search parties were sent in. Trained wilderness rescuers who knew what they were doing. We got maybe half of them back. Never did find the original science team. The state wanted to establish a full fenced perimeter barring entry, but there was never enough budget for it, so we've had people posted here, since this is the only access road in or out. This is my third summer working it, because it's an easy job no one wants and I think some of the history bits are fascinating. And while we turn away two or three groups every summer, there's at least one or two poachers or other folks who think they can hack it. We used to keep records," he said pointing to a folder on the map table that was as thick as a bible "but these days, we more wait until the missing persons reports come up."

"Wait, so what killed people down there? I'm missing that bit."

"In a way, the valley itself. Trees retook everything pretty quick after the draining, but a lot of houses got destroyed in the flood or collapsed afterward, so you have pockets in the ground that used to be someone's basement or root cellar, just waiting for a heavy enough footstep to cave in. Which is what we think got most people, then others would get hurt trying to get them out. And with the steep climb to get in or out of the valley, it gets hard to get to a point where you can be seen and rescued.

Plus, surface groundwater's still toxic, maybe even more so with whoever knows what got thrown into it during the flood, according to the readings taken outside the valley. It all gets filtered out underground past here where it merges with the aquifer, but it's definitely nothing you'd want to drink. And then, of course, there's the ghosts."

"The.. oh of course there's ghosts. Who am I kidding?"

"I'm not. Everyone who went in has reported shapes moving between the trees. Kind of thing you'd chalk up to paranoia if it was a few of them, but everyone? Something is down there, and real or not, if you get distracted by them, you'll wind up dead any number of other ways."

"Ok. Ghosts. Any wildlife or other, more real hazards?"

"Well, we've seen bear and elk move into and out of the valley at points, so you may run into either. Likely moose too, this far north, though I haven't seen any myself yet."

"Moose. Great."

"And then, there's the bodies."

"Bodies?"

"This wasn't a flash flood, exactly. No big plunging

wave that swept everything from one side to the other, thanks to the unevenness of the valley, the water went around most of the exterior first on this side, and then slowly filled in into the middle. So buildings didn't get knocked down, and people got trapped all over the place, inside and out, stuck as they drowned. Between the pressure and the cold of the water, the bodies, like the trees and a lot of the rest, didn't decay- they petrified, well, saponified. Fats and tissue hardening like soapstone. And since there's been no recovery work, they're still there."

"Okay, so, bodies. Creepy petrified bodies. Fantastic. That's still not stopping me."

"But you see why you can't go in, right? There is just no way to do this safely. You could just wait and catch him when he comes out, if he comes out. He's down there with no supplies, he's going to have to leave soon."

"Look, Cas? I've done a few wilderness pursuits before," Three, but he didn't need to know that part. "Every one of those is dangerous to begin with. I can be careful, but I have to go in after him. I'm being paid to bring him back, but I'm also supposed to be bringing back something he was carrying with him. I can't risk him losing it down there, or not coming back out at all, so better to go in while there's still some kind of trail."

Cas shrugged. "Look, until there's something

allowing us to let you in, you're not going in. Even if we did, if I thought I could stop you, I would. I've seen enough of these cases that it feels like assisted suicide, while we're stuck up here as witnesses. But look through everything here. Think it over. I need some water." He walked past me and out of the room. Not one to leave an invitation like that alone, I went over to the table and opened up the folder. Page after page of faces, photos from police and personal files, missing person reports, and the oldest in the stack, even Polaroids of the original survey team of seven people all in a group. Looking at the background of those last shots, I realized they were standing in this very room when the Polaroid had been taken, almost on this spot. A cold chill ran down my spine, and at the same time, the fax machine in the front room beeped into life, loudy printing in the otherwise silent room, shocking everyone into action. Charlie was the first one in there after me.

"That thing works?" He said in exclamation over the fax. Then he walked over to it and started reading the sheet it was printing out while it was still slowly extruding itself from the guts of the machine. Cas came back in a moment later, walking over behind Charlie. The moment the machine fell silent, Charlie ripped off the page, and turned it upright, reading it over again, before passing it to Cas. I simply waited.

Cas read through it, then put it down on the desk, and sat on the corner of the desk itself. Both him and Charlie were just staring at me.

"OK, how did you do it?" Charlie finally asked. "There's no way this makes sense."

"If you're going to accuse me of something," I replied. "I'd like to at least know what it is." Cas was hiding a chuckle or something behind his hand.

"Graft? Corruption? Government Conspiracy? I don't know what to even call it, I just want to know how you did it." Charlie replied.

"Did what?"

Cas finally broke the silence. "As of thirty minutes ago, you were officially deputized by the Stevens County Sheriff's Department. And since you're now technically state law enforcement, we can't do a damn thing to stop you from going in."

I was out the door like a bullet out of a gun, down the steps, into the Suburban and firing it up before the two of them even made it outside. I'll admit, there was a bit of an urge to screw with these two, so I actually revved the engine twice, hard, before putting it into reverse, and backing up around to the side of the forestry station to clear out the roadway, then parked it again, stepping out to go around to the back hatch. Cas came over my way, while Charlie went over to the barrier and started opening it up.

I opened the back door to the Suburban. I'd removed the final seat of the three bench seats in here to make more room for the equipment I needed on longer-term hunts. Given that I spent most of the year living out of this beast, it made more sense to keep most of it with me, rather than having to store needed gear at home. I opened the storage lockers built into the sides of the frame, starting to drag out the few things I'd need. Starting with the old frame backpack that was strapped up to one side. Checking it over, it still had everything attached that I'd set up after the last wilderness hunt— tent, sleeping bag, and bedmat were all still there, and inside were still the Sterno camp stove, toilet paper and other essentials, and ten MRE packs. I added in about a mixed dozen of protein and snack bars that'd do for breakfasts and lunches so I could save the more substantial packs for at night, then unhooked the two canteens attached to the frame, so I could head back inside to fill them up. Which is about where Cas caught up behind me, lugging along a heavy plastic case almost the size of a suitcase.

"That's not going to be enough water."

"No, but I've got purifier tablets, and gear to boil with."

"Neither of which will deal with what might be in that river. Look, telling you not to go obviously isn't going to work here—"

"You're right about that."

"—but I should go in with you. You don't have the experience for this kind of place, and"

"And you do? I thought no one was supposed to be going in there?"

Cas shot a look over towards Charlie, who was still dealing with the barrier, and I knew I'd guessed right— even if he wasn't admitting it yet, Cas at least had made excursions down into that valley. No one that obsessed with the place wouldn't have gone in at least once in three years of working it.

"OK, fine. Don't take me in with you. But look, we've put together gear for this, for the next time we'd have to attempt a rescue. You should at least take —"

"No. That's way too much stuff on top of what I already need to pack." I added a fifty-foot roll of climbing line onto the backpack from another one of the storage boxes, and then grabbed three pre-folded and rolled changes of clothes from another storage box. It might have been vanity to not want to smell myself after a few days worth of no changes, but at the same time, wet clothing

29

was nobody's friend on an expedition like this. Meanwhile, Cas had opened up the suitcase on the ground behind me and started pulling out items to hand me, the first of which was a slim, expensive looking metal case.

"All right. Here. Water purification handpump with a six-foot line. Unlike what you've got, this'll actually filter out the worst of what might be in the water down there."

"Thank you." I added it to the backpack, and then grabbed the smaller of the two medical kits I kept in the suburban and put it in as well.

"Don't you want a bigger kit? You get hurt down there, and—"

"If I get hurt worse than a few cuts, scrapes, or bruises, you've already made it pretty clear that I'm fucked for getting back out." I climbed up into the suburban to reach the first one of the locked strongboxes I'd had a friend back in New York weld onto the frame. Unlocking that I pulled out what was (for me at least) my basic fire kit— a zippo, a spare bottle of refill fluid, and a Ziploc bag that held a handful of strike-anywhere matches. Those went into the backpack as well. Then I shoved over the storage boxes on the floor to make room as I undid the two padlocks on the other main modification I'd had welded onto the frame— the gun safe. I propped the door of it open and did a quick mental inventory— four handguns, the old hunting rifle I'd inherited from my last set of foster parents, and a shotgun. The backpack was getting full already, and I didn't want a long gun getting in the way if I needed to run, jump or climb, so it was down to pistols. I pulled the 9mm Glock from the safe, still in its locking belt holster, and put it in the bag, along with a spare clip for it, then pulled out the Smith and Wesson 500 and the partial box of rounds for it I had leftover from the last time I'd field-tested and used it. The ammo went in the bag, and I set the gun down on the car floor while I dug deeper into the gun locker for something I'd had rigged up. Cas must have noticed because a moment later I heard the exclamation.

"Jesus. That isn't a gun, it's a cannon."

".50 caliber, just about the heaviest you can do and still call it a pistol." I finally found it— the custom holster I'd had to hand-sew it to make it work, but it fit around the chunky backpack strap just fine, putting the gun a few inches below my armpit. Better than getting a shoulder rig tangled up in my backpack, or having the weight throw me off carrying it on my hip or thigh. I held up the gun — it was the snub-nosed variant model that looked more like a police-issue .38 revolver on steroids, and then slotted it into the holster, where a heavy leather strap kept it in place. "You said it yourself

— there may be big game like bear or moose down there, and if I'm going to have to suddenly defend myself at close range, I'd rather be carrying the gun most likely to scare them off or drop them." What I didn't mention was that everything Wallace had done up to this point had me just as unsettled. While I was sure 9mm would stop him just as surely as the .50, I didn't want to take any chances. Regardless, into the backpack holster it went, while the partial box of ammo and the shoulder rig, just in case I needed to go without the backpack, went into the main storage space in the bag.

OK, that had the backpack most of the way together. Now to get changed, I went ahead and grabbed my shirt and lifted it off, then bit back a grin as I heard Cas stammer and turn around behind me. The sports bra I had on (pursuit habits over comfort when on the job) would do, but I wanted layers for down there in the shadows of the valley, so a blue, long-sleeve thermal shirt and a thicker black t-shirt over it. The joggers and sneakers I'd worn for the drive were quickly swapped for dark grey nylon ripstop pants, midweight wool socks, and a pair of hiking boots. Over that went my climbing harness— standard nylon webbing around the hips and legs, but anchored off on a heavy leather electrical lineman's belt that I kept a few other tools holstered on — specifically a small Maglite, a pair of handcuffs, and a collapsible climbing axe. Finally, the hair—box braids are good for keeping my hair down in something low-maintenance, but I didn't want to give the branches, my gear, or worse, Wallace an easy grip on me, so I spent a few minutes doing the necessary winding and twisting to bring the waist-length braids up into a tightly-packed bun at the back of my head.

I turned back around to see Cas still had his back to me and sighed. "I'm decent. Anything else you want to throw at me?"

Cas turned back. "Just two, now that I've thought it over." He reached into the open suitcase on the ground. "Flare gun, with a couple of extra rounds. If you do need help, it'll be the best way to signal. No cell reception down there, and our radios are spotty at best once you get deeper into things." I nodded and took it, adding it to the pile of gear inside the pack. "Also, radio," he said, handing me a medium-sized handset. "You should have partial signal at least up until you get into the buildings of the town itself. In case you need to communicate anything more detailed than a flare and you're clear of the town." I accepted that as well, stuffing it into the body of the backpack.

Charlie had finished with the gate and came back over to us at that point. "Are you seriously going in now? It's already past three. You're going to lose daylight before you even get very far."

"Still need to get as far in as I can on the route he took, try to set up my tent and everything as a base that might draw him in if he's in a state where that can happen. He'll be exhausted, cold, and hungry, so he might just walk up without thinking about it. I've had similar on a previous hunt. That said, mind filling these?" I passed my canteens to Charlie, and he dutifully took them and headed inside the station. I turned back to Cas. "Ok, what's the other thing?"

He pulled a sheet of printer paper that hand been laminated before it was folded up from his pocket and handed it to me. "Partial map. It's the original outlines of the town, pre-flooding, with a couple of edits from what notes we have from people. It's only good for the outskirts of town, though, we don't have records to show what's changed from age or damage towards the middle."

"Thank you." I tucked it into one of my pants pockets, sealed up the backpack, and hefted it. Heavy, but not so heavy that I'd be getting myself into trouble with a difficult load on top of things. The next several minutes were spent cleaning up the inside of the Suburban, locking everything back up, and by that point, Charlie was back outside with the canteens, which I gracefully accepted and stowed away— one inside the backpack, and the other on my belt. Then I shouldered the backpack, strapped it on fully, and that was that. Time to head in.

"We'll walk you as far as the wrecked car at least." Cas half-offered, half-stated, and I nodded. Keeping these two satisfied enough that they'd be willing to let me go off alone was easy enough, if I played things right, and the three of us walked up, over the crest of the ridge, and started down into the valley.

There was a steep bump at the transition from coming up one side of the ridge to going down the side of the other, and I could see in the unmarked dirt of the road the twelve foot gap just past that point where the rental must have been soaring for a brief moment before it finally hit the ground leaving deep wheel impressions, and the beginning of a sizable trail of oil and fuel— the landing must have gutted the undercarriage on top of things. Wallace was lucky the damn thing hadn't ended up on fire on top of everything. But the tracks fishtailed back and forth across the dirt and gravel for about fifty feet of forward descent following the road, until the road took a sharp turn to the right to follow the curve of the valley's ridge for a more gentle descent. The tracks continued forwards, past the road and into the twenty foot drop to the ground below. Looking down from the top of the drop, you could see the poor Toyota splayed out like a dead animal amid the thick tufts of plains grass and stunted trees that were all that grew in the shallow dirt of the ridgeline itself. It had landed upright, but both axles likely broke on impact if not before— all four tires were stuck out from it at odd angles.

"This is how you found it before, right?" I asked and both nodded. "Did either of you go down there?"

"No, we got the license plate when we were following it on foot, that was enough to record everything for the police and contacting the rental agency."

"OK, this is where we part ways, then. I don't need you two muddying the trail or going further from here. Just sit tight at the station, and if he comes out alone—"

"Stop him?"

"I was going to say shoot him until he doesn't move, but sure. Two days straight of driving, that drop, and he just gets out, closes the car door, and walks into the trees? I'm not looking forward to meeting this guy myself, and I don't think you two should take any chances if you do see him alone, all right?" Cas nodded, and I left the two of them there to follow the road as it turned, until I found what I was looking for— a spot where the drop turned into more of a shallow grade, which I half walked half gravel-surfed down to the same level as the car. Doubling back, I could see the two of them still up there, watching me. I waved, they waved back. Damnit, I was going to have onlookers for this.

The car itself was covered in dirt— dust kicked up from the road and from the impact with the fence and the ground after had caked it over in brown and orange, making it hard to see through the glass into the interior, but still, I swore I could see a small bit of movement inside, and instincts kicked in— I pulled my gun, and carefully circled around the front of the car to the driver's side door.

Definite movement inside— a large shifting mass of something in the driver's seat. I grabbed the door handle (thankfully it was unlocked), and pulled it open with my right hand, moving with the door so I could use it to partially shield myself. The door swung open for about three feet before the bottom corner caught on the ground and stopped, jarring itself out of my grip, which was also enough to disturb what was inside the car. I covered my mouth and nose instinctively as the giant swarm of bugs, what looked like flies mostly, though there were others too, boiled out of the car, rising up and out in a black column that reminded me of smoke as they began to disperse out in all directions. Beetles, centipedes, and other ground bugs plopped their way onto the ground from the drivers seat and scurried off as well. Coming around the door to look in, I could see the reason for all the insects

— the driver's seat itself was caked in a mix of stinking filth that I didn't want to think too closely about the source of, and was still crawling with more insect life to boot. The sheer number of bugs seemed excessive at the time, but I wrote it off to a rich environment, plus a warm, mostly sealed car. Pretty much perfect conditions for them.

Looking in without actually leaning into the car, I could see the rental agency's keyring still in the ignition, but no sign of the keys I was looking for. Then I noticed the folder on the passenger side— a thick manila number like you'd use for mailing paperwork, sealed shut. Loath to get any closer to the mess in the driver's seat than I had to, I went back around to the passenger side, only to find the door locked. I holstered my gun and brought out the collapsible climbing axe— still folded up so only the butt spike was exposed, a perfect tool for shattering safety glass. One quick strike, and I had the folder in my hands. I tucked it in behind me, between my back and the backpack frame where it'd stay in place for a bit and leave me with my hands free as I walked.

Walking around the back of the car I couldn't see any further signs of anything, just Wallace's trail where it continued down the slope. I took one last look up at the top of the road where Cas and Charlie still stood watching, then turned, and began to follow the trail deeper into the valley.

3. First Descent

They always talk about the descent as being the easy part of any journey like this. I'd love to find out who this "they" party is and make them take that trip down into the valley themselves. Wallace's trail was more than easy enough to follow— he'd clambered through everything like some kind of wildman, but once I hit the treeline, it was a series of sheer drop-offs from the ridge down into the valley floor. The original road that had led in and out had been a series of hairpin switchbacks going up the side, like a stepped terrace, and while the grade was still there, the original road had washed away, and two decades of overgrowth had filled it in to the point where rough greenery obscured the edges, and you'd find yourself almost walking off the edge of a six foot drop if you weren't paying attention. Wallace hadn't been for the most part— while there were times he followed the road, just as often, the trail would go plunging over the side, and I'd have to follow the grade around and pick it back up again where he'd landed.

Despite how many branches and plants he'd just crashed through, not to mention the number of times he must have just fallen over those little drops, I found no sign of blood, no markers that he was suddenly moving differently like he'd been injured or anything of that sort. Which was both good and bad in my book— an injury that slowed him down and made capture easier would have been nice, but at that point, I'd still hoped to take him in alive and bring him back out of the valley. Then again, I still didn't know how he was even capable of moving at this point— staying awake for a two-day-straight drive here from New York, crashing the car on arrival, and then just straight up walking right down into the valley— I was honestly expecting the trail to just suddenly end at a man that had collapsed into unconsciousness from sheer exhaustion or keeled over from a heart attack. But despite all of it, he just kept going, and the trail kept continuing.

The transition from half-hiking and half-sliding down the ridge wall to suddenly being on a flat valley floor had me stumbling as I finished the descent. But here was where the road finally turned off the ridge and entered into the forest that the valley floor had become, if forest was the term you could use. It was more like a jungle in some respects — dense growth, undisturbed by even heavy grazing, much less human hands. Everything had a sense of being crowded in as if nature itself was trying to cover up everything here with a dense barrier of plants. The decades since the flooded lake had been emptied was time enough for the pines, firs, and other evergreens that made up the bulk of the woods to almost reach full maturity, stretching up fifty, sixty feet to form a dense overhead canopy that blocked out the light. Here at the edges, though, things were more diverse, with bushes and plants forming a dense barrier around the edges of the trees that I would've needed a machete to get through, except for the remains of the road, which, barely bigger than a game trail at this point, led ahead of me into the trees. Thankfully, Wallace's trail went along the same path, though I was finding fewer signs of his passage as he kept to the flatter portion of the trail.

Fifty feet into the trees, and it was like I'd transitioned to another world, the sun and late September heat gone as the branches overhead filtered out most of it— the sweat I'd worked up on the descent chilled on the back of my neck.

The forest floor here was uneven, a thick, humped network of roots running just under the surface like massively overgrown veins and arteries, a network of stumbling points that ran around and between all the densely packed trees, all of it carpeted over with fallen needles and moss.

Here and there I also began to see signs of the much older forest that had stood here before the flood— solid black trunks of trees that had been drowned with the valley, branches sheared off by the flood itself or later currents, each one several feet thick and reaching up almost to the full height of the canopy. Coming across one near the trail, I couldn't help myself— I reached out and touched it— the cold surface of the bark gone from the hardness of wood and bark to an even harder state — these trees had all been caught somewhere near the petrification state by the sixty-year submerging in icy water, sap and resin hardening the wood partially into stone. That these hadn't broken apart and fallen since emerging and drying out like so many other petrified forests was probably testament to just how quiet and untouched the valley was by the outside world. As it was, the valley walls probably sheltered them enough from the wind to keep the breakage to a minimum, and the knotted roots of both the original trees and the new latecomers to the forest likely helped hold them in place further. But the overall effect, it was as if some alien cult had placed obelisks of blackened stone at random points throughout the forest, and no matter where you looked, you'd always see at least one of these spear-like trunks rising up from the ground.

The other thing that left me uneasy was the silence. In normal forests, you still had noise— the winds, birds, small and large animals moving through the brush, all of it added up in a normal white-noise level that at least told you that you were in a forest. Here, it was so much quieter, as if I'd set foot into a tomb. I could hear each one of my steps far more loudly than I should have been able to. My speed through the forest had also slowed down to a near-crawl. Between the closeness of the trees, the difficult footing around the path, and the atmosphere, I instinctively moved onto the defensive, eyes scanning around me as hard as I could as I continued. Half an hour of walking, uninterrupted, and I estimated I hadn't even covered a full mile of walking yet. Or even fully assessed some of the risks.

When I reached the first clearing I could see, little more than just a space just next to the path, I immediately stepped off the road and out into the open space, so glad to get a chance to see the sky decently and get a break from the oppressive air in the woods itself. But after a dozen steps I suddenly realized the danger I'd put myself into when I heard the hollow thumps of my footfalls and suddenly realized that the clearing was oddly rectangular. Echoing steps. Nothing that rooted deeper than grasses and weeds. I was standing in the middle of what had once been a house, walls and rooms swept away and destroyed in the flood and the regrowth after. And below me, separated only by what earth had been deposited on top of the rotting floorboards, was a drop of who knew how many feet straight into what would have been someone's basement or cellar. I slowly backed up the same way I'd come in, hoping that the ground that had held up for one set of strides would do the same coming back out.

And for the first two steps, it did, but on the third and fourth, I could hear cracking and snapping noises suddenly begin under one foot, then the other, and then I was running for the next pair of steps and jumping for the shelter of the trees as the ground began to shift. I hit the landing just a bit wrong, and found myself skidding to a stop back onto the pathway on all fours, gear swinging heavily around me as my pack tried to continue moving forward after the rest of me had stopped. Dust filled the air around me like smoke for a moment, but by the time I stood back up, dusted myself off, and turned around to see what had become of the clearing, it had already settled. As for the clearing itself, the corner closest to me was gone, a four-foot-wide hole that in this lighting was impenetrably dark. I let out a sigh of relief. First hazard survived at least.

Curiosity getting the better of me, I took out my flashlight and shone it down into the hole— a ten foot drop to a floor of stone. I could see part of a brick wall, though it looked like the mortar in between the bricks had given way to plants, dirt, and fungus. Piles of rotted-down wood, what must have been the remains of shelving, among other detritus, littered the floor. A smell wafted up from the opening— dirt, decay, must, the scent of things long since dead and moved on. As I began to turn away, a flicker of motion down there at the edge of the light caught my attention for a brief second, and I swung the light back down, and around, trying to see if there was anything else. Only the shifting shadows as the light changed angles moved back in response, and I finally turned away and resumed following the trail.

Half an hour of further hiking through the closeness of the trees. I saw two more clearings similar to the first, this time on the opposite side of the path. While the first one looked as untouched as the one I'd stepped into, something else had caused the flooring of the second to fall in— the entire clearing was still there, ground plants smoothing out any irregularities in the ground, just all of it was at the bottom of an eight-foot drop from the rest of the forest. I ignored both, since Wallace's trail just doggedly followed the road still. That alone had me impressed. He was still stumbling and floundering his way through the forest badly enough to leave a trail that had lasted for days, but he still hadn't so much as stopped to rest in any of this. I figured shock from the car crash may have been a factor at this point, but if anything it seemed to have made him blind to any kind of limitations rather than slowing him down.

The road widened back out, spreading into more of a natural clearing centered around a small stand of newer pine trees, and I was able to get some better bearings— guessing I'd come about three miles in total since reaching the valley floor. Meanwhile, the sun had already dipped down below the high northwestern ridgeline of the valley— while the sky was still light, it wouldn't be long, especially in those trees, before I was in darkness too heavy to safely keep going. And while the town itself couldn't be very far ahead, I couldn't take the risk of pushing my luck. Honestly, if I was going to set up a base camp that also acted as a trap point to draw Wallace in, this would be the spot.

On the southern edge of the clearing, I found proof that I wasn't the only one who'd decided this was a good spot previously— someone had dug out and laid down a few rocks to make a crude firepit, Though, given the level of dead leaves and other bits filling it, it hadn't seen use recently at all. Still, once I had my pack off, I took a moment to clean it out and grab a small pile of deadfall branches from around the clearing and got a decently sized fire going before starting in on the rest of the work.

Getting the tent and sleeping gear arranged and a pot on over the fire with water to boil up took only a few minutes— I'd had enough practice. What took more time were the extra details. Triplines set up on three sides of the camp, all of them low enough to blend in well to the ground. A bear bag weighted and bulked out with a few sticks and rocks as well as a couple of bells hung from a line that ran just a bit too long, putting it down in easy reach for a grown man. Beyond that, setting up further traps would have just been putting myself in danger as well, but these were enough, had done enough previously on one target I'd had to starve out of a forest. By the time everything was set up, the sun had truly gone down for the night— the pale-lit sky gone fully black.

I cooked. I ate. I wish I could tell you it was a beautiful heartwarming comfort meal had in front of a cheerily warm campfire that left me feeling nicely restored and ready to bed down for the night. It was an MRE. Even if you prepare them perfectly, there's always going to be something just off-kilter in terms of taste or texture that means while you may be full, you're never a hundred percent sure that what you ate actually qualifies as food. But full was a good enough spot to be in, especially when warm in front of a campfire and propped halfway leaning, half-sitting on a log. With rest as short-supplied as it had been so far, letting myself slip deliberately into a half-awake half-doze in front of the fire wasn't a challenge at all. It was a tactic that had paid off before— the supposedly asleep camper, supplies nearby and easily in reach for grabbing by a starving fugitive... honestly, if I was in Wallace's shoes, I'd have probably fallen for it.

But Wallace didn't. Hours passed on into the night, and before I knew it my partial doze became a full doze, and I was dreaming myself half-awake, lying just where I'd been sitting next to the fire that had burned most of the way down to dimmer coals and *something* was approaching the camp. A knot of shadows detached itself from the darkened bulk of the forest clearing around me and stalked forwards towards where I was lying. At first I was convinced I was simply lying in wait, like a good ambusher, biding my moment for when I could strike. It was only as it approached closer, and I could see the human-like shape of those shadows, that somehow walked comfortably on four limbs instead of two, and the way that the eyes were the only thing that caught the light of the firepit, reflecting it back as two pale circles of light, while the rest of it refused to show any detail at all, it was then that I realized that movement wasn't something I had any control of at all. I'd read about sleep paralysis before. But nothing had ever explained it on a level this vivid. I could feel everything as if I were fully awake, the ground and the log pressing into my back, the spreading chill as the fire died, and then that shadow—creature stood over me and reached out a single forelimb and with one extended appendage that was so like and yet completely unlike a finger it so gently touched my forehead and

I felt myself flung back and up over some kind of edge and then downward. Ice cold water, that's what I remember. The freezing jolt of being submerged so suddenly that your body goes straight past the shock response and directly into full pain, splaying out with every muscle spasming for a moment with the strain, and then just... floating there, in the void. Feeling the water all around me, lungs burning to hold onto what breath I could, eyes shut tight because for some reason I couldn't dare to look, as if looking would somehow make it all the more real. My outstretched hands reached blindly, hoping to find which way was upwards, and touched metal that was even colder than the water surrounding me, metal so cold it burned *and no sign of escape. Nothing but that cold metal up and down as far as I could reach. The trapped breath inside my chest burned as fiercely as the touch of the cold bronze in front of me, and while my fingers could feel some kind of carved shapes in the metal, there*

*was nothing to grab and pull myself upwards with, if
I could even find which way was up, I opened my eyes
and—*

woke up.

It was morning. The clearing was dimly lit, the
sun still below the eastern ridge, but the sky had
brightened enough to see by, and wisps of morning
fog had begun to rise from the forest floor. I'd
spent all night outside the tent, under the stars.
I rose and stretched, trying to shake off the last
of that nightmare, then grabbed a stick from the
rest of the deadwood pile to poke at the coals of
last night's fire, trying to see if there was enough
heat left to kick back up a full fire for a morning
pot of coffee or not. I nearly dropped the branch
when I saw it, just inside the edge of the pit in the
layers of old ashes I hadn't cleaned out previously.
What looked almost like a handprint, smaller than
my own, positioned right where the shadowy thing
from last night had been. I broke the remaining
cinders apart with the branch and scattered them
around the pit, trying to scrub it away. It had been
a dream. Dream monsters didn't leave prints in real
firepits. They also didn't have seven fucking fingers,
the one detail that I couldn't scrub out of my mind
as quickly as I scrubbed out that firepit. I could go
crazy later. Right now I was in a dangerous valley
with a dangerous fugitive to catch. There wasn't
time for this.

4. White Rabbit

After half an hour of repacking my backpack for a lighter load and breakfasting on another protein bar, and I'd managed to shake off most of the nightmare. My head was still stuck in that half-surreal sense that came from the general exhaustion of the chase so far, but otherwise, I felt I was about as ready as I was going to get for the next leg of this. On an impulse, I pulled out the radio Cas had given me, turned it on, and clicked the broadcast button a few times before speaking.

"Lake to… Forestry station? Station, anyone up there? Over." It's not like we'd gone over callsigns or anything. There was about a twenty-second pause that I assumed included scrambling for a receiver and then Cas's voice came through.

"Station to Lake, we read you. How was your night?"

"...you're supposed to say 'Over', when you finish talking, Cas. Or do we just not do signal protocol up here in the depths of nowhere?"

"Look, I turned this thing on for the first time ever yesterday afternoon. I think we're okay with skipping protocol."

"Yesterday afternoon? Cas, don't tell me you've been waiting next to the radio for me to call in all night." There was a long pause after that. Oh god. He *had*.

"...Okay, I won't." *Sure. Liar.*

"Okay, well, obviously, this isn't an emergency. Wanted to let you know I've made a campsite at a round clearing on the main path, about a half mile from the town proper by your map. Planning on leaving it set up while I go in further. I... uh." my hand encountered an unexpected papery object as I shifted the backpack— the manila envelope I'd grabbed out of Wallace's car yesterday. I'd forgotten about it in the rush to get on his trail.

"Uh?" Came Cas's voice on the radio.

"I'd found a folder Wallace had left in the wreck. Just taking a look through it now. Hang on." I undid the metal tab sealing the end and slid out a heavy sheaf of paperwork. Page after page of text records, all with the same Ravenswood Institute header I'd seen on the last check I'd gotten from them. No wonder it seemed like Hollowell had been withholding information— I was holding what was probably the Institute's entire file on Saltbrook. A lot of what I could read was similar to what Cas had already told me, recounting the poor history of the town, the flooding, and the reopening of the dam and explorations into the valley. Large sections of the reports were struck through with heavy black marker, though, redacting who knows how much information. And then there were the older reports, done on much earlier Institute letterhead, mentioning the "Church of Renewed Light," though these were even more heavily redacted than the later notes. The first page, labeled THREAT ASSESSMENT, was nothing more than two blocked-out paragraphs of black ink after the header. But it was the attached photographs that got my attention. Xeroxed sheets of photos, some actual sepia-aged photographs, others with that distinctive silver-gray tone of tintypes and older photography methods. There were a number of them, most of individuals like the portrait of an older clergyman wearing an outfit similar to a Methodist Reverend's collar and jacket. That one had a hand-inked label at the bottom "Reverend Fowler" and another of a young white woman, dark-haired, pretty, even if her posture for the photo seemed rigidly tense, labeled "Theresa Morgan-Fowler." Group shots of the church congregation (With Theresa and an older man next to her, presumably her husband, though I noticed he was wearing a suit rather than a clerical uniform — had she married outside the faith?) standing together in what looked like some kind of central stone plaza, a large well visible behind them to one side and the open doors of the church in the background on the other side. Another, older shot of the congregation in the plaza— no well, and a packed-earth ground instead of stone, the man next to a much younger, barely out-of-her-teens Theresa replaced by a much older Reverend Fowler standing behind her, hands on her shoulders.

There were other photos as well. Slice of life shots from a small town— several men in some kind of foundry space in work shirts and vests, pouring molten metal into a form buried in the ground. Three men, in suspenders, white shirts, and dark pants, standing between four evenly spaced trees, their backs to the camera. Crews leaving the mineshaft for the day, their clothing and tools covered in dust and stains. A mother and children eating a picnic lunch. Brick and stone houses and shops on a narrow main street of bricks. One shot of the church itself, probably one of the biggest buildings in town— a multistory construction of rounded river stones. Though I did notice one odd detail there— wherever I expected to see a cross or crucifix on the building, it was a design more like some of the Celtic crosses I'd seen— a quartered circle, the bottom arm stretching downwards further than the rest.

I thumbed the radio back on, "Well, Cas, when I come back up, I've got stuff for you to copy for your historical collection— the file had a bunch of old photographs in it among other things, stuff from back before the flooding."

"Anything interesting?" he replied.

"Actually, yeah. Old photographs for one, but I'm wondering if you can look something up for me, too, see what you've got on the Church of Renewed Light? A lot of these files mention it, but they've blacked out big chunks of it."

"I don't remember anything off the top of my head, but I'll look through what we have here. Anything else?"

"Should do for now. I'll have the radio with me, but I'll be keeping it off unless I need to contact you. Going to head into the town now, follow the trail. I'll contact you again tonight if I haven't found anything."

"All right. Be careful. Station over and out."

"Over and out." I switched the handheld off and put it back into my bag. Then I re-sealed the files and stuffed them under my sleeping bag, shouldered the now lighter backpack, and stepped out of the tent.

The fog that had been just starting to rise up from the forest floor when I'd first woken up had thickened, forming a thick white curtain between the trees that was only just starting to burn off in the full morning sun coming over the valley. Beyond that, the campsite and the clearing were just as I'd left them— silent. Eerily empty.

And yet, as I straightened up, I could see it, just in the corner of my vision. The same image I'd seen in the photographs a moment ago— three male figures, standing evenly spaced between four trees on the far edge of the clearing. I blinked, turned my head so I was looking directly at the north side of the clearing, and they were gone, but I swore I'd seen them in that moment. As it was, there were still the trees— four of the old drowned trunks from before the flood, as perfectly spaced out as if they'd been planted that way. I walked over for a closer look, but there was nothing at first glance. No crushed plants, no prints, no sign anyone had stood in those places in decades.

I've pushed myself to the limits of exhaustion before this. You have to in most survival training, just so you know what your body and mind will try to pull on you when you're in that state. While it had never pushed me to the point of hallucination before this, it was still just barely enough within the realm of possibility that I finally just shrugged it off as sleep deprivation, mentally filed it away with every other thing that had been off thus far, and started back in on following Wallace's trail.

Five minutes back on the path and I may as well have left the clearing behind on another planet— while the fog was starting to burn off, it was still more than thick enough to screen off everything fifty feet ahead or behind me, while the trees themselves formed barriers to vision on either side. The path itself curved northwards as I continued on, the trees pressing closer in until the broken brick path was little more than a game trail, with broken and root-tumbled bricks to either side, making the footing even more treacherous. At the same time, there were more signs of the old town to either side of the trail— more of the house-sized clearings and sinkholes like previously, followed by ones with first floors still partly intact, corners and walls looming up out of the ground caked over in decades of lake sediment until they looked more like partial sandcastles that had since been melted by the tide.

And then, looming up on my right, was the first almost fully intact house I'd seen. A Victorian design, built almost entirely out of stone and brick. The layers of sediment that remained stuck to the visible parts of the first floor giving the whole building the appearance of some kind of spiky house shaped growth that had pushed its way up out of the ground rather than that of a manmade structure. None of that was what had caught my eye, though. Sunlight was filtering down into the valley now, and a brief ray of it had caught on something bright yellow near the front of the house, and even though Wallace's trail continued along the path ignoring it, I felt I had to go in for a closer look.

As I pushed past the trees and ferns that littered the ground, I could see the entire front steps that led up to the entrance of the house had caved in, and I could see the source of the color that had grabbed my attention— a chunk of nylon fabric, faded from an intense yellow to more of a pale canary, stuck in between two boards that made up part of the jagged edge of the front porch at the top of the hole. I took the Maglite off my belt and shone it down into the gap. The drop was a good twelve feet into a basement or a root cellar, and there, at the bottom was the remains of another explorer. Time and what few scavengers there were to be had around here had already stripped the flesh away and turned clothing, broken wood, and whatever organic remains it could into fresh dirt that even more of the ferns were beginning to sprout from. But, you could still see the frame of a hiking backpack similar to the one I wore now, the yellow fabric torn where it crashed through the hole. Polished bone reflected back the light at different points— pieces of a skull, arm bones twisted and broken to one side, a jumble of ribs around the base of a fern. There was no telling what had been an injury from the fall or later damage from the scavengers, only that the fall itself killed the person, as they hadn't even moved away from what must have been the initial impact. At least it had been quick for them. I turned around, not daring to get any closer and risk a second collapse, and headed back for the trail.

The walk gave me time to think, which I both did and didn't need right now— Wallace's trail was still just as old as the sections leading up to where I'd camped which meant he'd done all this in one solid stretch from the car accident onwards, and it was beginning to strain the limits of what anyone could've done, shock or no shock. At the same time, all the little details from the files, the forestry station, all of it kept percolating through my head. What was so important to Wallace to drive him like this? What's the importance of the church here? Some historical find? Buried treasure lost in the flood? There wasn't evidence of either in the records. Where did the keys that Hollowell wanted to recover tie into all this? There were just too many questions and it felt like I had none of the answers at this point. It all felt surreal, as if I was missing entire reasons for why all of this was happening the way that it was.

Which of course is when I arrived at the town proper, or rather, at one of the entryways in. This was one of the few markers Cas had added to his map, just an arrow, an x, and the note "root tunnel" in blue ink. Though coming up to it, I would have been pressed to think up a better name myself. A pair of four-story brick and wood buildings stood opposite each other here, with the forest making walls of its own right up to the walls of the buildings. While the trail continued between the buildings, widening back out a bit to be more like the old road that it actually was, the entire wall of the building on the left had broken free, falling whole and outward until it hit the building on the opposite side of the street. It must have happened after the flooding with the water to cushion the impact, because otherwise I couldn't imagine a scenario where that wall didn't collapse completely to the ground instead, but it had somehow stayed up all this time, the lake depositing a thick layer of muck on top of and around the sides of the wall that pressed it down further, but also strengthened it, leaving an angled-roof tunnel almost the width of the street and with what looked like eight feet of clearance at the beginning. Strangest of all, though, trees grew on top of that damaged section of wall, stunted a bit, but looking healthy, and their roots had worked their way through the wall and the muck, hanging loose in the open air of the tunnel, like a threadbare curtain. Some of them ran all the way down to re-root themselves in the tunnel floor, but most didn't quite have the length yet. This was going to be slow going, but Wallace's trail went right up to the tunnel. I could only assume he went through. Hopefully, he wasn't waiting for me somewhere in the middle.

As I turned on my flashlight, I noticed one other detail— someone had gone to the trouble of cleaning part of the corner of the undamaged building where it met with the tunnel, and they'd added a bit of decoration of their own— eight feet tall and done in a style so hyper-realistic, I almost expected it to twitch a whisker and go sprinting off through the tunnel ahead of me, was a white rabbit. No, not a rabbit so much— the artist had an amazing eye for details, and the lean muscularity, the hardness of the ear and madness of the red-ringed eye... it was a hare. An albino hare. I also noticed at that point just how new the painting was — the lack of dust, or any sun fading or weathering, this had to have been done in the last couple of months at the oldest.

I looked at that graffiti, and then to the mouth of the tunnel that the rabbit was poised to go sprinting down, before saying: "The name is Alicia. Not Alice." And then down into the rabbit-hole I went.

The tunnel itself could only have been about a hundred feet long. Maybe three hundred at most if it was the entire block that had fallen over. I could see dim, filtered sunlight at the far end of the tunnel. I kept telling myself that as I cautiously walked ahead. I had one arm up and out in front of me, warding off the hanging roots, and I'm not ashamed to admit the other hand had drawn out the heavy weight of the .50, keeping it down low to my hip. I'm not normally claustrophobic, but this place was getting the better of me. The roots were thin and sparse at the beginning but before I'd gotten a good twenty steps in, they thickened in both size and number, and instead of pushing aside hanging tendrils, I found myself pushing myself through what felt more like hanging netting that had been shredded by a former captive. The feathery, dirty-moist touch of the branching rootlets was everywhere, tickling its way across my skin, and the light just kept reflecting back from more and more of the tangle as I pressed ahead rather than showing me anything useful. I paused, reholstered the gun so I'd have my other hand free, and blindly pushed forward. Wallace had done it. I could do this.

The tickling touch of the roots became more of a full-on drag as they thickened further. Roots as thick as my little finger would catch and drag on my arms, legs, and the edges of my pack before pulling free or sliding aside. Everything was so close and hitting my face so often that I closed my eyes and just kept pushing forward blindly. My imagination started becoming my worst enemy as I kept trudging forward through the clutching vegetation, supplying me with imagery of me suddenly getting not only caught but fully stuck and trapped in the roots, slowly choking as I became more and more ensnared in them. Or worse, that my reaching hands would suddenly find not more roots or soil, but the softness of rotting flesh, or the hard curves of bones. Thankfully, none of that happened, and after another minute or so of flailing forwards, I could feel the grasp of the roots lessening, and the curtains becoming thinner and thinner. I risked opening my eyes. The end of the tunnel was just ahead, maybe fifteen feet away, screened off by only a thin layer of the remaining roots. I took one struggling step ahead with what felt like the entire network of plant matter from the tunnel dragging at my pack, then another, and then I was suddenly free of all resistance and falling forward from momentum. I caught myself on both hands and just knelt there on all fours for a moment, dragging in deep breaths.

Looking up and to my left, I could see the graffiti artist had made it through as well— they'd left a companion piece to the hare at the entrance to the tunnel, only this time the rabbit was upside down, back hunched in a spasm of pain as it disemboweled itself, luridly painted entrails lifted up and out of its body by its hind claws to drip red gore down onto the white fur. It was just as disturbing as the original, and just as amazingly executed, but after the tunnel I wasn't in much of a mood for art, and the thought of the gore set my stomach churning.

Turning away from the paintwork, I slipped my pack off and dusted it and myself down from the extra layers of dirt that I'd picked up in the tunnel. The roots, where they'd been damp from the morning fog, had left behind odd patterns over all of my clothing and the pack— mazes of lines and streaks like a city map drawn up by a drunken cartographer. Most of the staining wouldn't budge, but I at least got the loose stuff knocked off of everything and out of the inside of my shirts before re-shouldering my pack. With that done, I finally turned around slowly to take stock.

I...there is no easy way to describe the town as I saw it just then. Some of it was what you'd expect

— there were buildings, a north-to-south running main street which I stood at the south end of now. The buildings themselves were what you'd expect for the time— brick and stone, most of them single-story but some going to two, three, even four floors further north of me. The street itself was made from hand-laid brick. Just a touch wider than a modern one-way lane. There were storefronts with large display windows, restaurants, all the hallmarks of a small American town stuck decades in the past. But that was where the similarities ended. Like the rest of the valley so far, you could see the effects the flood had had, only here it was less a case of how the flood had damaged things, and more how it had shockingly preserved them. The buildings at the edges of town took the most force of the initial flood waves, leaving many of these here in the middle intact— sure, there were broken windows here and there, but few, if any, of the central buildings had been caved in by the pressure— it had had time to slowly build as it drowned, giving brick, stone, and timber time enough to take the weight where it would. Debris and mud drifted in with the water, and silt settled down over all of it with time, encasing the buildings in layer upon layer of mud and earth, the weight of the water compacting and compressing all of it together. And then all that water slowly drained away. But here, out in the middle of the valley, where wind, sun, and rain could reach and touch everything unimpeded, they worked like a fine set of brushes and tools in the hands of a skilled archaeologist, paring back the layers of encrusting earth, clearing the tops of buildings, the surface of the street itself, but leaving flows of that dirt intact, like veins and arteries of the valley itself supporting the upper reaches of buildings while the lower floors remained partially to fully encased, especially where surfaces were rough enough to help it grab hold. In essence, the feeling that the town had just grown organically out of the floor of the valley was still very much alive.

And yet, it was so still. No breeze currently blew through the leaves of the few saplings growing out of the earth collected at the base of the hat shop to my right. No one walked through these streets, despite the remnants of what once must have been a horse-drawn cart to my right, the bed, free of two of its broken wheels, canted upwards at odd angles to the ground. More important to me at the time, though, was one key fact— given the weather-swept nature of the ground, with barely a layer of dry dirt over brick, the path that Wallace had left in his wake was gone. I was out of trail to follow with a whole town ahead of me, and no clear leads to go after. Which meant following some unclear ones instead. All the documents he'd stolen mentioned or were at least tangential to the church that fronted onto the plaza at the north end of town, and it was as good as anywhere else to start, so I began making my way up the road in that direction.

The first two blocks of travel northwards were undisturbed. The silence was as thick as a blanket, which, I suppose is why I nearly jumped out of my skin when a low grunting noise in the distance to my right that turned rapidly into a higher-pitched whining howl of noise broke through it. My gun was out and in my hand on instant reflex at that point even before my brain had had enough time to register just what the sound was. Elk. Early in the season for a mating call, but still, just a normal animal sound, even if the echo made it impossible to tell if he was just blocks away from me, or out in the deeper forest. He was probably the only one in the entire valley, or I'd have heard or seen signs previously. Still, I made a careful point of looking into the distance at the next intersection, instead of just at the ground and buildings for signs of Wallace's trail— it wouldn't do to run headfirst into a startled bull elk when they're at their most territorial.

Thankfully that level of care let me see one thing I needed to see— an open door. It was on a building on the south side of the cross street, about halfway to where the street ended and more forest began. A squat two-story brick structure with a flat roof that had since begun to sprout trees of its own, but in the noon light, the doorway was visible as a simple rectangle of pitch black in the exposed front of the building. It wasn't exactly on my way, but it was worth checking. I took the turn and walked over to it. The building itself was an L-shape, surrounding an open yard that might have once had play equipment in it before the flood, though now it was just open ground that wild grasses and a few sparse trees grew out of. The sign, near the open door, had been stripped of any paint by time and weathering, but the thick wood still had the rough-cut letters nailed to it, just barely rising above the dried-on silt and mud that had covered it— "The Saltbrook School." Of course the population hadn't ever gotten big enough to bother with splitting grade levels, much less anything more original of a name. Below that, someone had also nailed on a rough-cut symbol— a circle, quartered by a cross, the bottom arm longer. A sign of solidarity and faith, or a hint that the church had helped or run the school? I wasn't sure which.

More importantly, there, not ten feet in front of the door was a wide patch of bare ground, soft enough that it had taken shoe prints in both directions — Wallace's trail. He'd come through here at least once, though no telling just how long ago.

I swear I heard *something* as I examined those prints. A sound from just inside, a roughly drawn breath, or a light scrape on wood. Something. Peering inside, well, it was a school's entry foyer.

The layer of dust and mud on the windows meant it was almost pitch black in here. I took one step inside and blinked a few times, waiting for my eyes to readjust to the gloom. I was glad I'd taken the time to wait. The floor ended only four feet past where I stood, the inside ground floor of the building having collapsed into the basement. Looking up, I saw it wasn't the only one that had seen such damage— large chunks of the second floor had fallen through as well, leaving that basement a chaotic jumble of debris.

Whatever might have been in here, there were no signs of Wallace having the tools to get down into the basement, much less back out again. I assumed he'd done what I was about to do— turn around and leave. But as I did so, I heard that sound again, that rough indraw of breath, behind me, to my right, followed by a series of short exhales, muffled, near-silent. Someone behind me was *crying*. I turned to look, and there in the gloom, I could make out a bare, rounded shape, pale white skin, the curve of a back hunched protectively over something in the corner of the wall near that front door. I must've nearly tripped over them when I came in, only how could they even be here? Still, some things life ingrains in us so deeply that we respond without thinking. I felt sympathy. Concern, even. I took a step towards the hunched figure, that I was sure was sobbing in a feminine voice. I reached out a hand, touched an ice-cold shoulder. "Ma'am?"

The crying shifted, sped up, gaining in volume as it shifted from constant sobs to hysterical, desperate, laughter as the shape turned and lunged at me. I saw in that brief instant eyes that were nothing but reflective voids, no iris, no white just an impossible mirror-brightness in the dark room, and a mouth so brokenly unhinged that it couldn't have shaped the sounds I heard, and then it hit me and I felt a cold dampness as it passed through me, disappearing into the darkness of the room. I turned back. The curved shapes still sat in the corner, grey and unmoving as if they'd been carved out of stone. I brought out my flashlight for a better look.

I almost thought they were mounded rocks at that point, between the grey color and a visible texture that looked more like wax or stone at first. But then my eyes started making sense of the shapes I saw — the curve of a shoulder here, the line of a spine there, and as I worked my way visually around to see the side that was facing into the corner and the ruin of a face above all of it, and the two forms huddled in front of it. Not just one body, but three. Saponified, like Cas had warned me about— where the water, cold, and pressure had not only prevented decay from setting in on those who'd drowned in the flood, but preserved them in a way that would defy decay and scavengers for decades to come, cooling and solidifying the fats and liquids in a corpse and forcing them out to cover the surface in a waxy layer that shielded the rest of the body underneath. A woman, likely a teacher here, protecting two of the children who hadn't been able to make it out.

If not for whatever I'd seen just a moment before that, it would have been sad and touching, but as it was, I had had *enough.* I was done with this town, this search, this everything. I walked out of that school fully ready to turn back out of whatever the hell this was turning into, going back through that tunnel, and *leaving.*

So of course the minute I walked out the door and turned left to go back to the main street, I saw a male form, limping, but moving at a walk so fast it seemed more like a dead run, through the intersection and north towards the central plaza and the church. Wallace. It had to be. Every trepidation I had left me. The prey was in sight, and it was almost over. He was already out of visual range, so I set off at a fast walk to follow.

5. Confrontational Discovery

I took my time in following Wallace— mostly because that plaza was open ground with several directions to run in, which was the last place I wanted a confrontation. What I needed was to catch him unaware, or inside a building, better yet, both, just so I could cut down on his options if he didn't decide to come along peacefully. And given how everything else had gone thus far, peacefully was the one option I was betting against — this guy was going to resist capture and resist it hard. So I opted for stealth for the moment. As I approached the intersection with the main street, I moved to the north side of the cross street I was on, pressing close to the building at the corner and dropping low to peer around the corner. Looking up into the plaza, I could see him, walking from a low structure that had to be the well in the middle of the plaza eastward, towards where the church should be— I couldn't see the church itself since it was set back from the plaza by a bit of distance, but I gave it a short count of thirty seconds, letting him leave my view entirely before I came around the corner myself, walking fast to cover the last block between the intersection and the plaza.

The plaza itself was a short step up in height from the rest of the street, probably to make sure traffic flowed away towards any one of the four different roads that met here, constructed from river rocks instead of the brick used for the roads— if it weren't for all the silt and mud that had been permanently packed in between each stone like an extra layer of mortar, It would've been like walking on a rough dry streambed, but as it was, the surface was smooth and level. It was just as quiet and empty a place as the rest of the town— the benches, cans, and other features that should have been part of this were it still a living town had been swept away long ago, leaving it an empty plain, aside from the well.

The well itself was massive— what had been laid down as a four foot tall octagon of mortared natural stones, first rounded by nature and the river before the construction, and then, with sixty years of water swirling around it to reshape it, the surfaces had been polished down, swirled until the individual striations of mortar and different types of rock resembled more the branches and whorls of veins and nerves in muscle, all rendered in varied shades of grey and black. It was beautiful, if more than a little odd and distressing, all at the same time. The smooth drifts of dirt that had piled against buildings in town were thinner across the plaza in general, where moving currents would've helped to keep it clearer, but there were still piles of it drifted up against the sides of the well, and Wallace's footprints went right up through those to the front of the well, before turning away across the plaza towards the church.

I followed the marks right up to the smoothed stone, and instinctively laid a hand on it. Despite the sun shining down into the plaza, it was still cold, almost painfully so, and as my hand laid there for a moment, I swear I felt a momentary pulse— a thump of movement, like something hit the stone from underneath, sending vibrations through it. I froze, hand still on the stone, waiting, but no other vibrations followed. Looking down into it, between the already odd angle of the sun, and the high walls, I could only see about seven or eight feet or so down the well shaft before it all disappeared into shadow.

Standing there, hand still on the well, is when I noticed the other main feature of the plaza, beyond the well and the buildings surrounding it— the oak tree— situated to my immediate right about twenty feet away, towards the corner of the church, just barely on the church grounds itself. It was the first one of the petrified trees I'd seen in the central portion of the town, likely because the town itself hadn't left many trees behind in the construction. But this one... this was a truly massive oak, one that must have been hundreds of years old before the flooding had ultimately killed and petrified it— the trunk, a giant lumpy thing that curled back on itself before stretching upwards had to have been a dozen feet thick, And while most of the branches had been sheared away during the flood, or fallen and broken under their own weight after, what few remained stretched up into the sky, almost past the height of the church. More disturbing though was what I'd first mistaken for an odd t-shaped pattern of staining running up the front of the tree trunk, and all too quickly realized was another one of Saltbrook's many corpses.

She (the form was definitely feminine, even despite the bloating and distortion that had occurred as the body saponified, turning it into another of the rock-hard mummies like the others I'd seen previously) was standing fully upright, back against the tree trunk, arms spread wide behind her, the distance between them around the trunk bridged by a rusted length of heavy iron chain. Unlike the other pair, her skin had been stained a deep reddish brown by the alkaloids in the water, darker than my own, even, though the most fascinating thing about her was the pose. I knew it had to be just the way gravity and the currents had let her drift down a touch, but the way her upper torso leaned out from the tree, but her head fell back towards the trunk again, the jaw dropped open and held in place by withered, hardened tissues... it was like her entire body was voicing one final scream of defiance up at the sky.

A flash of something at her throat caught my attention, and I found myself stepping even closer to look. While her clothes were gone, either absorbed into the petrification or shredded and lost to the water, the silver chain of a necklace still hung around her neck, blackened and tarnished where it wasn't fused into the mummified tissue. Carefully, I pulled up on it, trying to see what was hanging at the end— a pendant, a quartered circle, the bottom arm of the cross twice as long as the others, covered in faint traceries of decorative lines, that had somehow resisted the tarnish that covered the rest, so similar to the symbol I'd seen on the church and carved into and adorning so many of the buildings here. There was a tug on the chain, and I looked up, horrified to see the woman's head tilting down towards me, eyeless sockets moved to look directly into my own eyes for a moment. Then the head turned further, snapping loose of the chain that had been fused to it, and falling free of the body. It split when it hit the ground, one chunk of forehead falling away from the rest, petrified flesh and skull breaking apart into what looked more like random rocks than anything that had ever been alive. At the same time, I could swear I heard the noise of wood splintering and breaking coming from inside the church. Wallace. Without thinking, I shoved the necklace into a pocket and drew my gun.

Wallace had gone through the double doors at the front of the church. Given the sounds coming from inside, I didn't want to go in the same way and potentially walk myself into an ambush. Thankfully, I didn't have to— one of the largest deposits of mud and silt I'd seen yet was piled up against the south side of the church, ending just a foot below one of the windows on the second floor. I circled quietly around the building, slowly walking up the shallow grade of the hill of lake residue. The drift was mostly firm footing— only the top inch or so had been loosened by wind and dry weather, so it was more like walking up a snowbank than anything else— that peculiar step-slide of gaining and holding footing that exhausted leg muscles all too quickly, but in a short minute I was at the top. The window frame itself was intact, but the glass had shattered long ago from water pressure or some other accident, giving me a clear entrance, save for a few jagged splinters of glass sticking up from the bottom of the frame. I took the extra time to pull them from the wood and toss them down onto the hill— the last thing I needed was an injury now— and then bent and ducked in through the window.

I was on some kind of mezzanine level above the nave of the church. Well, I don't know that they called it a nave, but I'd been raised in enough Catholic homes to immediately think of it as such. I was on a wooden catwalk that extended to my left into a larger platform, probably for additional seats or for the choir or who knows what above the front entryway. The mezzanine extended across the width of the nave, and there was a catwalk on the opposite side as well. Steps led down to the main floor to my right from both catwalks. Or they would have, but on the opposite side, something had broken through, shattering those stairs. That must have been what I'd heard outside. And then I heard a heavy tread beginning to ascend the steps on my side of the platform. He was coming up here.

I moved quietly and quickly, ducking around the corner of the railing to the main platform behind the rails, nearly tripping over the remnants of broken pews in the process. There, crouched low, I unholstered the .50 caliber pistol, yet again, and got my flashlight ready in my hand. Wallace, meanwhile, was taking his time with the steps. He must have fallen through the first set— I could hear him carefully testing, then stomping on each stair before moving up to the next. I started to keep a careful watch at the top of the steps— catching him there, with some good distance between us seemed like the perfect setup. But then movement flickered down below me, and I couldn't help but look.

The floor of the church was stone— carefully polished slabs, swept clean by the floods except for the broken debris of pews to either side of the room, but the thick steps leading up to an altar carved from the same stone were still fully intact, and it was in front of those that a tableau began to play out before me.

It was like some projectionist had begun an old black and white film playback down there in what little gloomy light filtered in through the broken and grimy stained glass windows. A figure, a woman, pacing back and forth in front of the altar, somehow dimly glowing with her own pale light, though it seemed to wash away any color there was to her at the same time. When she stopped pacing and turned to face the doors, I recognized the homespun dress as well as her face from the photos I'd already recovered from the car earlier— Theresa Morgan-Fowler. Drowned and lost decades ago. Even more, I recognized the silver necklace around her throat that even now seemed to be burning like a lump of pure coldness in my pocket. She'd been the body outside the church, still chained to the tree.

A man was coming in from outside, in the same pale, glowing condition as Theresa. While I couldn't see his face from the angle, he was wearing what seemed to be the ubiquitous uniform for men around town in that era— a light-colored work shirt, dark trousers, suspenders, and a wide hat.

"Is it done?" Theresa asked him. Apparently, these ghosts got the full audio playback perks as well. I don't know how I knew, but I was sure this was just a looped performance, that these two had been doing this for years now.

"It's done. The charge blew as predicted. We've got three hours at best, but the flood's already coming in. Between that and the rains, it might be less. A lot less."

"We work with what time we have, in His grace." The man bowed his head in response. "Go send people out to get the others, we need every person who agreed to guard a winding point in place. And send word to the rest of the believers to gather in the plaza. We'll meet our—" she broke off, coughing into a handkerchief, even paled out as everything about both of the apparitions were, the stark redness of blood showed against the white cloth. She resumed— "We'll meet our fate together as the first ones to walk into a new paradise. Go."

The man turned and started to leave through the front doors, but stopped when she called out. "Steven! One more thing." he came back to her side, as she pulled a bulky pouch from off the altar. "The keys. Once you've done the rest, get out while you still can. Come back when it's time. You'll know when."

"Dubrovsky said ten years."

"We can't trust that. When the floodwaters recede. When God shows you, you'll know. Now go, before you run out of time."

"I will." He replied. "I'll—"

"*Go*, Steven. I'll see you in our new paradise." He turned and left. She resumed pacing.

I was so entranced by what had been going on below me that I'd missed what had moved right up next to me until I heard someone suddenly, raspingly inhale just to my right, as if he hadn't been using his lungs this whole time until now. I recoiled, sidestepping left, clicking on the flashlight by habit and turning both it and the gun on Wallace at the same time.

Saying he looked terrible was an understatement. Wallace had been a six-foot tall, heavily overweight white man in his fifties. Now, he looked— I don't know how to sum it up, but in the moment of turning the light on him, all sorts of small details hooked their way into my mind. Like how the skin sagged off his frame as if he'd burned away everything but tendon and bone as fuel in his flight. The absolute filthiness of him— the suit he wore that, like his skin, now hung off him like a circus tent was stained with all manner of foulness, and this close you could smell the reek of excrement, decay, sweat, blood, everything a body could put out in one disgusting cloud of stench. He was pale to begin with, but he now seemed almost bloodless, the sagging skin nearly translucent. Dozens of small injuries— scrapes and scratches on his hand, arms, and face oozed small dribbles of blood, but showed no signs of healing or closing up. And then his face— jowls hanging loose, marked with dried spittle and blood, teeth coated with foulness, eyes fixed on me but stubbornly refusing to shrink back down from being so dilated that you could barely see the brown ring of iris around the pupils, even despite the harsh glare of the flashlight. A deep cut ran across his forehead, but the blood barely oozed out of it.

"Enjoy the passion-play below?" He asked in a hoarse rasp, the sibilants sounding almost like a lisp— his mouth wasn't even wet enough to make the right sounds. Later, I'd put everything together and be horrified. Right now, it was compartmentalized— locked away in another part of my brain while the bounty hunter side had reflexive control of my mouth and hands.

"Frank Wallace, you are under arrest per New York bounty law. Put your hands up."

"No." He took a step towards me, and I immediately sighted his right shoulder and fired, the boom of the .50 caliber round thundering echoes off the inside of the church. I was done with chances. The force of the blow knocked him back, off his feet. I took a step closer, planning to turn what had been a disarming into a double-tap, but as I did, he was back up and moving faster than anyone should have been able to recover from a hit like that. He grabbed the still-hot barrel of the gun, twisting it half out of my grip as he turned me so my back was against the railing. One-handed, but his grip and strength were like iron. I could see the hole through his shoulder where I'd shot him, see through exposed muscle and bone, none of it moving or pumping blood save when he consciously moved, to the wall behind him as he reached up with his other hand. I dropped the flashlight and grabbed that hand by the wrist, but it was like trying to stop the tide as he slowly, inexorably, laid two cold fingers on my forehead.

"Not yet, little hunter. You have so much more to *understand,* first." There was a little *tap* of pressure against my forehead from those fingertips, and then the aged rotting wood of the catwalk railing gave way behind me, and time seemed to slow as I was falling back and over the edge towards the stone below, Wallace standing there above me, waving with one hand before starting to turn away.

6. The Plunge

I was falling in slow motion, Wallace, or whatever it was that had been Wallace waving at me and turning away also in slow motion, and then it was like everything changed. I kept falling back, but even as I did, everything around me moved like a slow-motion time-lapse film in reverse. The railing I'd just broken through flew back up and reassembled itself. Wallace faded from view, but all the little details of damage from the flooding and time itself started undoing themselves, more and more rapidly. The windows cleared, cracks filling themselves back in in a blur. Dust faded, but at the same time, just as suddenly I could see the waters rising up outside the church, the light shifting and changing color until everything was bathed in a dim blue-green glow of sunlight filtering through deep waters. I could hear the sound of wood shifting across the stone floor, and looking to one side, I could see the pews reassembling themselves from splinters, dragging themselves across the floor into their original positions. I landed softly, on my back, on a carpet that hadn't existed on that floor a moment before.

"...and the Lord did send forth His rains. For forty days and forty nights he sent them!" It was a female voice talking, even if the sound had first started up like a cassette tape slowly picking up speed until it was suddenly playing back the audio at the right pace. I picked myself up and stood there, in the center of the aisle between the rows of pews as the voice continued to speak. "And those floods were sent to the people as both a scourge to the wicked and a test to the faithful of the Lord, our God. So too are we being tested even now, my brothers and sisters." There were *people* here. Well, not exactly people, and not a lot of them. About a dozen, sparsely packed into the three front rows of pews nearest the altar. All of them had that same flickering, here-and-then-not aspect to them that I'd seen previously, the colors of skin, hair, and clothing leached away like black and white photos left to fade. Between them and the altar stood a woman, more solid-looking than the rest though still faded. Theresa again, though here there were fewer lines around the corners of her eyes, less grey at her temples. A Theresa at least a fe years younger than what I had seen before Wallace knocked me over the railing. It was her talking, of course. She continued: "And that is why I have called you here together for this prayer meeting. We are being tested today, even now, as the city council takes up their vote on whether or not we will be staying here in our valley, in our new Eden as promised to us by the Lord."

No one here seemed to even notice that I'd fallen into the middle of their little prayer meeting, including Theresa, who'd looked right through me a few times. I shrugged, stayed standing where I was. Playing the fly on the wall suited me fine right now, and I already had the feeling that this, whatever *this* was wasn't going to end until I'd seen whatever it was that Wallace wanted to show me.

Theresa continued: "Let us pray, brothers and sisters. Let our voices be heard by the Lord that he might make change in the hearts of the town council, that they—" she broke off as behind me, the church doors opened and closed again, and a blurred figure ran into the church quickly enough that with the fading and flickering I couldn't see any detail whatsoever as they ran down the center aisle, passing through me like I was the one who wasn't even there.

As it hit my chest and ran through me, though, I also noticed another detail I'd missed in the fall — my clothes. At some point in the transition to whatever this was, my clothes had changed— I was wearing the same outfit I'd seen on most of the men from the old photos— woolen pants with suspenders, a button-down work shirt, and heavy shoes. My pack, and all my gear, appeared to be gone. Great. At least it wasn't skirts.

The blur continued to run past me, right up to Theresa, where it stopped long enough to solidify into a teenaged boy, who quickly whispered a message in her ear. The congregation had their heads bowed already, they didn't see the look of pure rage and frustration that crossed Theresa's features for a moment before she recovered and put on the face of a serene pastor once more. "I need you all to excuse me for a moment. I have to go to Town Hall. Brother Randolph, could you continue to lead our circle in prayer while I'm gone? I won't be but a few minutes." One of the pew-sitters nodded in agreement, and then all of them, including the messenger, everyone but Theresa faded out of existence. The church itself became a much darker place immediately, lit only by the glow of the water outside the windows. Theresa herself began walking up the aisle towards me, and I stepped into one of the pews to avoid getting walked through again— it didn't feel like anything, but nevertheless, the idea itself wasn't all that pleasant. But she kept walking out of the church past me, and, lacking an idea for what else to be doing, I followed her. Once out the doors, she immediately turned right, heading north just up to the street at the end of the plaza that led over to the Town Hall from what I remembered of Cas's map. I, on the other hand, had to pause.

I'd stepped out into a completely different world than the one I'd been in when I entered the church. The same dark blue-green glow suffused the air like the town was still submerged, though I walked and breathed normally. The streets were free of mud and earth, the buildings repaired as if the flooding had never happened. Ghostly flickerings moved up and down the street, occasionally resolving themselves into a person looking into a shop window, neighbors tipping hats to one another, a group of children playing in the plaza, and other remnants of what had been normal life here. And all of it was dead silent. No sounds of wind or water, the only footfalls I could even hear were my own.

I turned to look north. Theresa was already getting ahead of me, a good half-block distant, and I hurried to catch up so I was only a few yards behind her. As I did, I noticed it wasn't just her I was following, at least, not exactly. Like the other people I'd seen, she was flickering as well, only with each flicker, it was different versions of herself

— younger, older, different clothing, different hair. As if she'd made this journey so many times at so many different ages that they all blended into each other.

I put my hands into my pockets, trying to appear nonchalant, even though I knew on some level that no one was paying any attention to my presence, and my hand encountered one item that had made the transition to this place when my own equipment hadn't— the silver necklace I'd taken off Theresa's corpse outside the church. Despite being deep in a pocket it nearly *burned* with cold, like a chunk of ice. My hand felt like the cold was about to send it into a cramp, and that's when I noticed that Theresa had stopped moving. The flickering shifted, becoming a downward motion that took her from a more youthful version of herself, shifting down through several years of age at a time until it suddenly stopped her looking much like she had when I'd first entered the church. At least, from behind. I noticed in my peripheral vision that every other ghostly flickering loop of a person had also stopped moving, everything becoming absolutely still. And then Theresa's head began to turn back towards me. Slowly, inexorably, I had the sudden instinctive feeling that whatever happened next, her face was the absolute last thing I wanted to see at that moment. I took my hands out of my pockets, looking for cover to duck behind, and the moment my finger lost contact with the necklace, Theresa, and every other one of the ghosts, flickered again and continued forward as if nothing had happened.

So, at least I had a way of getting their attention. If that was something I wanted to do at all. Right now the option seemed downright dangerous. I didn't know what the rules were here, or how I was going to survive this. With that in mind, continuing to follow Theresa seemed like my only option, so I did.

The Saltbrook Town Hall was a three-story brick building, built on what seemed to me to be an overly ambitious plan for a town so small, but then again, hubris and an assumption of growth always seemed to be the prevailing attitude here. Decorative wrought-iron fencing wrapped around it at the ground floor, and at the top of the first story, since the higher levels were set back a bit from the front. The entryway, however, was open, the gates swung back and locked in place to either side with chains. Theresa paused inside the fencing for a moment, bowing her head in every flickering iteration of age for herself. I stayed outside the fencing, but I reached out to touch the gate, wanting to feel something solid in all this. Instead, the iron bars distorted in my hand, rust spreading out from where I touched, the framing twisting to show where something had rammed into it, bending the bars. The rust spread lightning-fast from my touch, covering the gate and spreading into the fencing in a matter of moments, whole sections of the fence crumbling away as I watched in horror. I let go of the gate, and the spread of the rust stopped, about twenty feet away from the gate. It didn't show any sign of magically undoing itself, though. The damage was done.

Meanwhile, Theresa had finished up her prayer, and was stepping through the doors— passing through them just like the messenger in the church had passed through me. As soon as she was through the door, I reached up a hand to touch it— solid to me, and I could see cracks beginning to run through the painted wood from where my hand contacted it. Not wanting to do as much damage as I had to the fence, I hurriedly grabbed the knob— the door swung open, and I let go and stepped inside.

The lobby was more of a landing here. A granite counter with a door just beyond it that led further in on this floor, one stairway going to the left, and another stairway going down to the far right. Theresa had paused again a few feet inside the door, and as I watched, she *split,* the different-aged versions of herself going in separate directions — the youngest staying on this floor, older going up, and the oldest taking a hurried, fearful look back towards the door and then turning to head downstairs.

Not sure which to follow, I went with the one

going downstairs, if only because of that look back before Theresa had gone that way herself. Her age, clothing, everything then was a match for what I saw in the church before Wallace had pushed me. This had to be something from the day of the flood. I figured that had to key into all this somehow. The walk down the stairs was short, and I quickly came face to face with a closed and locked metal door that Theresa must have just walked through. On impulse, I grabbed the knob and held onto it. The layers of paint on the door went through what seemed to be a rapid onset of water damage and aging, all spreading out in waves from where my hand gripped the knob. The door aged decades in seconds, the rust-covered knob and lock breaking off in my hand. I reached a pair of cautious fingers into the hole left behind and pulled, the door sticking in protest at first, but then swinging slowly open on its now-rusted hinges. And then I walked through it into an altogether different kind of nightmare.

It was clear now that the bottom level had been built as the town's jail, though I imagined it was more for holding prisoners for transport to larger cities to await trial. Still, the hallway had six iron-barred jail cells here, three to each side. Theresa had already walked through the length of the hallway, passing through a wooden door at the far end, leaving me without the ghostly glow of her presence for lighting. Instead, I had other light sources— there was a glowing presence behind every single cell door. How a town this small kept a full jail was beyond me, but some of these cells even held multiple ghostly images, flickering through all the states of being prisoners— lounging against walls, leaned up against the cell doors, sitting in the corners or lounging on the beds affixed to the walls. All of which changed as I walked down the hallway. As I walked, I noticed it happening in every cell— some of the ghosts rushed the doors, some of them stayed put, but all of them stood up, some standing on the beds or even the toilet. Others rushed the bars, sticking flickering limbs through that were too hazy to be easily recognized as hands and arms.

By the time I was halfway down the hall all of them began to rise up off the floor, and that's when I realized what was going on. Whatever bastard had been in charge of the evacuation had filled the jail and left them there, and that door I'd gone through was solid, but not watertight. Like everyone else left behind here, these ghosts were caught in a loop in time, right up through their own drowning. I watched, transfixed. I couldn't help but feel some guilt over their fate, some need to somehow free them so they could escape, but what could I do? They had died decades ago. And even now, they were dying all over again, rising up with the water levels, until each one was held up near the ceiling, and then kicking, struggling, thrashing involuntarily, and then their lights flickering out into the darkness— some went faster than others, but before I knew it, only two were left and I knew then that stuck in that empty jail in the dark waiting for the ghosts to possibly return and die all over again was the last place I wanted to be. I continued on through the door, hoping to catch back up to Theresa.

The door at the end of the cells was thankfully unlocked and I went through it into what had been a storage room of some kind— nothing remained on the rows of heavy wooden shelving that filled the room, so I had no idea if this had been meant to be evidence storage, or files, or some other police or jail related business, or something completely different, but there was only the one door and no sign of Theresa at first. Until I realized that there was more light in the room than just the dim floodwater-light filtering in through the single window high on one side of the room. Flickering white ghostlight was leaking in from a crack in the far wall, following the lines of the wooden slats that made up the wall itself. Not seeing any kind of handle, pull, or catch, I gave a light push on the section of the wall itself and was glad to see it swing inwards on oiled hinges.

The room beyond was down a bit, offset lower from the rest of the basement level of the town hall. And it was shorter, with a lower ceiling, on top of that. A tiny, weird room of crude stone walls, like it had been tunneled out and finished as an afterthought. But the oddest things weren't the room itself. Even with three of those flickering ghostly figures packed into it. No, it was the log. A massive wooden trunk took up the back half of the room, hanging parallel to the floor. It filled the space floor to ceiling, and I couldn't tell you how long the trunk actually was, because the far end extended past this room, going down a corridor at the back that looked like it had been specifically carved into the earth to admit it. Ropes as thick as my arm tethered it, presumably, to the ceiling, though those also extended up that corridor away from here, at almost as horizontal an angle as the log itself, and a heavy iron eyebolt and chain were anchored into the visible end of the wood, the chain winding back into a slot in the wall between the rocks. If the chain was released the whole thing would swing down and away from this room, but to what purpose, I couldn't guess at the moment. Besides, my attention was focused on other details in the room at the same time.

As I'd said, not just Theresa, but two more of those ghostly, afterimages from the past were here. All three were positioned around a stone plinth that had been built into the floor near the same wall that the chain hooked into. The plinth itself stood only about two feet off the ground, with a broad top that rose at a slight angle from the floor. Set into that top was a wheel, like the locking wheels used to seal bulkheads on ships or similar. One of the two figures with Theresa had just finished turning it when I'd come in— I recognized him as the man she'd handed the pouch of keys to back in the church, though to be fair, I more recognized him because he had the pouch out and was pulling a ring of keys out from it to insert one into the lock at the center of that wheel. The key turned with an audible click, and as he turned the keys over in his hand to put them back in the pouch, I was sure I could see one on that ring that was larger than the rest, with a brassy finish that barely showed against the flickering ghost light. So. Hollowell's stolen ring of keys. The one thing I had to recover from here even if I didn't bag Wallace.

Theresa turned and spoke to the man who wasn't holding the keys. "Now, Anthony, I need to ask this. Have you come here of your own choice, by your free will?" He nodded. "No, Brother Anthony, I need you to say the words. You have to say these out loud. Have you come here of your own free will?"

"I— I have." He replied in a voice still partway cracking with puberty. Damnit, what the fuck were they doing? He was still practically a kid. This whole thing felt like some kind of cult ritual.

"You agree to guard this post with all your strength?"

"I do."

"You agree to stay here, for as long as you are needed, even in death itself, until the day when the bell is sounded and the Lord lifts us up into salvation?"

"I will."

"Thank you, Brother Anthony. Now, kneel as you were instructed." He knelt down in front of the plinth, leaning back so that his own back rested across that top surface, blocking anyone from reaching the controls. A rope appeared on the floor, as if it hadn't mattered enough to this scene to be visible until just now, and the man with the keys grabbed it, feeding it through a pair of eyebolts on the floor, and then binding each end of the rope to one of Anthony's wrists, stretching him back even further and holding him in place. Theresa meanwhile stood in front of Anthony, unbuttoning and opening his shirt. Once his chest was exposed to the cold air of the room, she pulled out a small flask from one pocket of her dress and poured a small measure of some kind of liquid over two of her fingers, which she then used to draw a cross-like shape across his chest.

"You are sealed and anointed as the watcher of this

station, Anthony. The Lord, and I, will not allow you to falter."

"Amen." was Anthony's response, which was echoed both by Theresa and the man with the keys as he finished his knotwork.

Theresa stood back up and turned to the man holding the keys, passing him the flask of oil. "Thank you Thomas. See to the others and perform the blessing if I don't arrive in time. I'll catch up as I can, I need to make sure they've started in the plaza already." He nodded, and both her and Thomas faded away into nonexistence, leaving me alone with the tied-up Anthony and my own thoughts.

My mind was still racing. The keys that Wallace had, that were his whole reason for coming here. They were obviously meant to operate the mechanism they'd left Anthony (and others, remembering that there were four standard keys on that keyring) guarding. But what did the mechanism do? Did the fifth key, the one made out of brass do something different? What was all this *for*? Solve that, and I'd know what Wallace was really after. And knowing what Wallace was after would make the second attempt at bringing him down and getting those keys back that much more possible. I still wasn't going to try and even explain to myself what had happened with that last attempt, or how he had still been moving. But none of that was here. Here and now, I needed to find out Wallace's trail in all of this, and I had the tool to do so.

But as I watched, Anthony's body suddenly started rising up. I'd hit the flooding point in this replay of history, and just like in the cells, the floodwaters had invaded this room as well. Unlike the prisoners, though, poor Anthony was still tied to the floor at the same time, and only rose a few inches up off the plinth he'd been resting on. I could've looked away, but honestly, I felt that if I was going to have to indulge in morbid curiosity this much, I at least owed it to him to bear witness to what was going to happen. So I was looking right at his face when he finally opened his mouth. There were no visible bubbles of air rushing out, but there was the oddest expression of surprise on his face. Like he'd been expecting to hold out longer against the waters. Then the thrashing started— a full kick followed by all four limbs getting into the act as reflexes kicked in, trying to somehow, anyhow, get free and get to the air, even though there surely wasn't any left in here by that time. And then, stillness— the body still slightly buoyant, just hovering in the air at the ends of the ropes, a few inches above the plinth. The bent-backward pose, head pulled back by gravity, seemed almost serene, angelic, made more disturbingly by the slightly parted mouth and the lack of strain or expression on the rest of his features. The flickering light of Anthony's ghostly presence faded away, leaving me in a room that was only dimly lit by some kind of residual glow.

It wasn't enough. I knew Wallace would be interested in this room, but what I really needed to know was if he'd been down here already, before I'd caught up to him. If what I thought about the fence and the door had been true, then... without thinking further I reached out and placed my bare hand on Anthony's dead torso, just to the right and a bit below the sternum.

It was like time itself spread out from my hand, rippling through the corpse in scattered threads like veins, spreading and spreading so rapidly I could barely track it, the flesh on the body expanding slightly, then tightening down onto the bones like shrink-wrap, forcing fats and other fluids out to the surface where they hardened in the cold of the water. I couldn't feel any of it through the hand I had on the body, just a cold chill, so cold my hand wanted to cramp up into a fist, but I forced my fingers open, *pushed* into the contact I had on the body. The effect picked up speed, and spread further, down into the ropes, the woven hemp expanding with absorbed water, darkening, blackening with age. The darkening of age and settled muck from the water spread across the floor, darkening the stone a touch more. The dim room grew even darker.

Anthony's face and details of his features, even individual bits, like fingers were gone now, wiped away by the expansion of the saponification that had turned him into what looked more of an awkwardly crude statue than a human corpse. Four rough limbs and a rounded mound of a head, all attached to an irregular torso. All of it looked more like crudely cast concrete than anything that had been flesh or bone. Except where the ropes cut through it, showing bits of yellowed ivory at the partially exposed wrist bones. The room around us had dimmed to where my vision could barely cut through the darkness any longer, except for a remaining dim glow from where my hand was pressed into Anthony's body. The saponification had risen up around it, layering almost all the way up the side of my hand. I wondered if there'd been more fat in his body if I'd have found my hand encased by the petrification. Before I could do much else, though, the body slowly settled fully back onto the plinth, the stretched and thinned ropes going slack.

I took a deep breath and almost removed my hand from the body, but then it shifted once, bucking slightly under my hand, and before I could even finish that breath, the torso suddenly broke free of the limbs and flung itself at the far side of the room, like someone had just reached up and kicked it out from under my hand. It was only lit by the glowing palm print on the body from the side of the room, but I could still see the surface of the plinth and watched as the slot for the key abruptly turned itself ninety degrees with an audible click. A sharp vibration ran through the floor, like something had suddenly sprung open, though there was no visible change beyond that— the log and chain still hung in their place, the room didn't shift or look any different, nothing else. Still, even without seeing him, I had my answer— Wallace had already been down here. Whatever else he was doing here, the machinery the Church had left behind was part of it.

With nothing else to turn up in the way of a clue here, I turned to leave, thinking I could pick the trail back up top in the plaza or some other part of the town above me. I noticed the rapid aging effect from my touch was still fully in effect here — I wondered just how far through the building it had spread as I took a step onto one of the rounded, mortared-together stones that made up the flooring, and the mortar crumbled away at the weight of my foot, taking both the stone and my leg downwards. Other stones and whole chunks of the floor gave way as well, falling away below me into darkness. I lurched forward, hands clutching onto the edge of the concrete stairs as more stones fell away under my weight.

There was a long moment of silence, ended by the

distant splashes as the heavy stones struck water far below me. I may not have been able to see how far the void beneath me stretched, but I knew falling was about the last option I wanted to do, and while I had a solid grip on the stairs, ten fingers worth of grip on a flat concrete surface wasn't going to last long— I was already starting to ache from the strain. I wasn't sure about my strength to keep my grip and just pull myself up directly, so I started a move I'd done in a few rock-climbing gyms on overhangs where I didn't have the leverage to pull myself straight up; a slow side-to side swing. A few passesof swinging my legs from left to right to build up momentum, and there— on the fourth swing I had enough speed built up— I pulled up with my left arm and popped my entire right arm up onto the step above the one I'd had my fingers on, bracing myself up onto the concrete up to my elbow. At the same time, I curled myself in around the empty space around the step, bringing my leg up, trying to get my right knee up onto the same step. I got my leg up over it for a second, but then the cloth of the trousers I was wearing instead of my hiking/climbing gear tore on a sharp corner edge as it slipped, and I felt the tearing pain on the inside of my knee as it gouged through, followed by the jerk of my shoulder and arm taking my full weight again as my leg slipped off. But with one arm up, I pulled up and forward with my left, getting that arm up over the top of the stair as well, onto the second step. Half my weight on the stairs now instead of hanging over it. I was hurt, but at least I could just grab and drag myself forwards and up out of the pit, which I did.

From the top of the steps, I turned to look back. Some threads of the past were starting to fade back into the room, restoring the look from before I'd touched Anthony's body, but the damage was still there. A yawning L-shaped pit, the floor completely fallen away from the stairs up to about a foot away from the plinth, and then curving around towards the back of the room, where the log was anchored on the right. The stone floor didn't look to be coming back, and I could only wonder if the damage existed in the real world too as well as this... dreamscape? Vision? No, this wasn't time for introspective thoughts about the nature of where I was— this was time for getting the hell out of this building before any more floors gave way, so help me.

Back through the storage room, I seemed to be on more solid footing at least, though the room was still shot through with threads of age and decay, the plaster crumbled down to the floor in raggedly torn sections, showing exposed lathe and brickwork behind it. Most of the shelves were crumbled to debris on the floor. But even as I watched, I could see bits and flecks of plaster floating up from the ground like a reversed time-lapse video of snowfall, quickly starting to fill in the gaps on the walls at the edges. I didn't waste time watching the restoration work, instead, I braced myself and pushed ahead into the jail.

The aging effect from my touch hadn't spread as far as the jail. Or it had already fully receded back out of the room. Either way, it was done with, as was the replay of the drowning of the people who'd been trapped in here, and their eventual decay and the draining of the water. The prison was stained dark gray, with even darker blotches where walls held residual water, and in each one of the still locked cells, rounded shapes littered the floor at odd angles— the petrified remains, distorted from age and movement, left behind in nearly unrecognizable pieces— the curve of a shoulder here, the distended split branch of a leg there, tibia having become disconnected from fibula to stand out at an odd angle. Flickering afterimage ghosts appeared in fits and starts next to their former bodies— just blurred shapes of light with no detail or clarity, here one moment and gone the next. I hadn't seen the ghostly loops extend past what had been their death before this, and inspiration struck me.

Like before with Theresa, as I moved to the middle of the corridor running through the jail, I reached a hand into my pocket and grasped the still ice-cold necklace I'd taken off Theresa's corpse.

Immediately, every flickering half-there outline reformed with razor clarity. I could see faces. Men, women, with a turn of my stomach I realized two of them were teens barely more than children. Every last one of them clear and sharp and colorless as if they'd been black and white photographs, still wearing the normal clothes they'd had on when they'd been imprisoned. Every last one of them fixed and turned to stare directly at me with eyes that looked like jet-black marbles had been placed in their sockets instead. I took a step back involuntarily, and their eyes and faces tracked with me, following every move.

"Can— can you see me? Can you hear me? Understand me?" I asked. And all of them opened their mouths in wordless unison, filling the air with a cacophony of clicking, scratching, whispering noise like the combination of a swarm of locusts piling over a thousand furious chalkboard writers. I reacted instinctively again, pulling both hands up to cover my ears, breaking my contact with the necklace, and the ghosts flickered back into their half-existence. I started to move to leave, but as I did, a half-remembered detail of what I'd just seen grabbed at my brain and I stopped at the edge of the cells. I turned to look back again and grabbed the necklace in my pocket. The ghosts all reappeared, lined up against the bars so they could stare at me, but still somehow unable to violate their imprisonment.

I studied facial features, clothing details. Black. Asian. Noses and cheekbones that looked Native. Curly hair peeking out from under a skullcap. The two teen boys in separate cells yet still arranged so they could be close to each other as possible and still look in my direction. I don't know what charges may have been trumped up to put them here, but with a sinking twist to my stomach that almost brought tears of anger to my eyes, I knew why they were really here, and why no one had made a move to save any of them when the waters began to rise.

"I'm sorry for what they did to you." I remember saying. "If I can, I'll fix this." I let go of the necklace and turned and left the jail through the still open door before they could make any kind of reply.

Up the stairs and out the door— no sign of Theresa or any other flickering loops yet, even outside. Maybe everyone's time here had run through except for mine, I'd thought, until I turned the corner to re-enter the plaza.

They were all here. Dozens of the ghostly flickering all in the plaza, more coherent than the ones in the jail, but all of them dressed in their Sunday best, gathered together as families, singing hymns I couldn't hear. They stood between Theresa, where two of her helpers were lashing her to the trunk of the old oak in front of the church with a length of chain, and the bulky mass of the well. She lifted both hands from the chain, and the hymn-singers fell silent, looking at her with rapt expectation.

"It is time, my brothers and sisters. Can you hear that?" She paused, and even I could hear it at that point. The rush of water. "The Lord is upon us, and he shall sweep us up into his keeping, all too soon. And all as I have told you, as we of the Church have planned, the Lord shall give us his grace, and after a time, we shall live here again, in this Eden we have constructed. Hold fast, brothers and sisters. Show no fear in what is coming next, for we shall be restored when His great bell rings out across the valley!"

Between everything I'd seen including and especially the jail, I'd had enough of this. Without thinking, I grabbed the necklace out of my pocket, my hand cramping into a fist around it with the increased cold. When I did so, I suddenly felt a cold wetness, and looked down to see the actual floodwaters, dirty brownish black, tipped with white froth, already reaching above my ankles as well as everyone else's here. All the flickering ceased, and just like the jail, eyes turned to pitch black, as each and every one of the ghosts turned silently to face towards me.

"This is bullshit!" I yelled at them, putting myself

between Theresa and the massed crowd. "She is lying to you. They've all been lying to you. The floods come, and you all die, and that's it. That's all that happens! You're dying for nothing but an empty promise! None of you survive, or come back! There's nothing!" I noticed the water was now up to my knees.

As one, the crowd in the plaza opened their mouths, and again, that horrible clicking scratching noise filled the air, amplified so much more loudly by all the extra mouths joined into the chorus. I turned around to face Theresa. "This is your fault. You killed all of these people for a goddamn myth!" I was going to throw the fucking necklace at her at that point, but as I swung my arm, my hand simply refused to open, still bound up with the cold of the necklace somehow. And then looking past Theresa, past the church, I saw the massive wave of the full floodwater coming. The wave broke on the trees behind the church, splitting to either side of the building and sweeping down into the plaza onto all of us. I felt myself picked up by the waters turning around and over to see the ghosts quickly flickering out of existence as the too surged up with the water, somehow becoming part of it. I felt myself flung back and up over some kind of edge and then downward, into the only spot the waters would go down in the plaza, into the open drain that was the well.

Ice cold water, that's what I remember. The freezing jolt of being submerged so suddenly that your body goes straight past the shock response and directly into full pain, splaying out with every muscle spasming for a moment with the strain, and then just... floating there, in the void. Feeling the water all around me, lungs burning to hold onto what breath I could, eyes shut tight because for some reason I couldn't dare to look, as if looking would somehow make it all the more real. My outstretched hands reached blindly, hoping to find which way was even upwards, and touched metal that was even colder than the water surrounding me, metal so cold it burned and no sign of escape. Nothing but that cold metal up and down as far as I could reach. The trapped breath inside my chest burned as fiercely as the touch of the cold alloy in front of me, and while my fingers could feel some kind of carved shapes in the metal, there was nothing to grab and pull myself upwards with, if I could even find which way was up, I opened my eyes and saw nothing, just darkness crushing down with all the cold iciness of the increasing pressure as the waters rose ever higher above me. My mouth opened involuntarily and I could feel and see the air rush out of me in one burst of bubbles, rapidly replaced by cold water rushing down my throat. My entire body spasmed again, and my hand finally opened, the silver cross falling away from my touch, except where the chain was wrapped around my thumb and—

7. Exit And Recovery

I woke up convulsing, jerking upright, head bumping against the nylon of the tent as I coughed up dark water all over myself. Hands grabbed at me, and I instinctively lashed out with a fist, followed by another fit of coughing up even more water.

"Woah, woah, it's okay. You're okay. You're all right, try and breathe." a familiar voice, I turned and looked and was surprised to see Cas, from the ranger station in my tent looking at me all solicitous.

"The fuck are you doing here?" I managed to spit out between fits of coughing. I was soaked, drenched in far more water than I'd coughed up, my neatly folded sleeping bag and bedding under me damp with it. I was wearing the clothes and harness I'd hiked into Saltbrook with, though my backpack wasn't on me— I could see it, propped up in the far corner of the tent, thankfully still dry. Despite the punch that had left a nice fat red mark on Cas's cheek, he immediately hovered into close view again, all too overly solicitous right when I needed to catch a breath.

"Are you okay? Can you breathe? How do you feel?" Damnit, the kid was practically shotgunning me questions. "Can I—"

"I. Need. TO. BREATHE." I enunciated around a raw throat. "Back off a second." He thankfully did, moving back as far as the inside of the tent would allow. At the same time, I suppressed a shiver— if nothing else, even the water that I was sitting in was still cold as ice and it was starting to get to me. I started taking stock out loud as I got off the wet bedding. "Cas, I just woke up half-drowned, and I'm freezing, but otherwise I'm not—" there was a twinge of pain as I shifted, and I realized that the scratches and bumps I'd picked up under Town Hall and in the plaza were very real and very much still with me. "OK, I'm a little hurt, but not seriously. Bumps and scrapes. Now back to my question— what the fuck are you doing down here?"

"It's been three days since you radioed us last, so when I finished the night shift this morning, I came down into the valley to see if there was any sign of you or anything to recover. I got here about half an hour ago to find you lying on top of your bag, unconscious, and not waking up for anything. I was getting your fire built up and looking for your radio to call in medevac when you suddenly woke up, soaked in water that hadn't been in your tent before this! What the fuck is going on?"

"I— I don't know exactly. OK, look. I'm starting to freeze from all this. You got the fire going?" He nodded. "Good. Hit my supplies out there for some food, start something heating up, I'm going to get changed. Give me a minute to get all this settled." Cas nodded again and left the tent. Three whole days gone. It didn't make any sense I thought to myself as I stripped off my wet everything. The clothes went in one sodden pile while my soaked boots, my remaining gun, and climbing harness went in another— I'd need to get those dry before anything else happened. As I was getting everything off, my hand encountered the cold lump of Theresa's necklace, still in my pocket. That went in the pile with the boots.

At least the backpack had a full change of everything and was dry, even if it was the gear designed more with the thought of late fall to early winter in upstate New York. Right now I needed the warmth anyways. Once I got shirt and pants on (and did my best to avoid thinking about the waterlogged bun of box braids at the back of my head, that was going to have to be its own full salon visit once I was done with this), I pulled the pile of boots and soaked gear out of the tent. Cas had, thankfully, also gotten more wood in the process of building up the fire, and I used some of the thinner deadfall branches to prop up the boots, harness and holsters at the edge of the firepit. Hopefully, they'd dry out enough to be usable fairly quickly. As I turned to go back into the tent I noticed immediately how dirty it had gotten— that mix of staining that happens from condensation, loose dirt and dust, and any kind of breeze when you're out camping. Not that I doubted Cas, but it was good to have some kind of corroboration that I'd lost that much time.

Back in the tent, I grabbed the cleaning kit, spare 9mm rounds and the Glock, and then went back out again to sit down at the campfire and actually warm up now. Cas handed me one of the remaining MREs, a full canteen, and sat back, poking at the fire with a stick while I nearly inhaled the contents of both— now that I was waking up, both hunger and thirst were starting to hit. Thankfully Cas was polite enough to remain quiet until I'd finished with both to start in again with the questions.

"All right. Let's say my disbelief's been suspended ever since you summoned up ten gallons of ice water in your sleep. I'm ready to believe just about anything, but before I get into the stuff you had me research or anything else, what *happened* in there?" I took out the cleaning kit and my gun, spread the piece of deerskin I kept in the kit for exactly this purpose across my lap and started field-stripping the Glock. A wet gun could mean serious injury or worse in the field, and I already knew I was going to have to go back in.

"I don't know exactly what happened, Cas. I know the events. I know what I did, I know what was done to me. But it's like putting together a puzzle when all I have are the pieces that make up the frame. I'm missing too many pieces to see what the picture is." My hands worked on automatic, running a cloth down the barrel with a rod to clean it out before field-stripping the gun down to its component parts.

"Nice thing about having the frame, though, you can see what parts you need. What'll eventually fill the hole." Cas replied. I nodded back, and began detailing what, to me, had been the last day or so. While I talked, my hands worked. For a gun that was supposedly pretty water-resistant, moisture had managed to get into every crack and crevice of every part of it, even the clip. I dumped the rounds in there onto the ground and grabbed a second dry cloth from the kit, glad I'd packed extra. By the time my hands finished getting every last bit of moisture out of the clip and had started on oiling and reassembling the rest of the gun, I'd managed to cover all the way up to entering Town Hall. I paused, went into the tent, and came back out with the box of fresh ammo I'd packed, slowly and steadily reloading the clip. When I mentioned falling through the floor, Cas's eyes widened noticeably, and I had to pause again.

"Cas, there's no way that that part could be real, right?"

"Well, that's the thing. Parts of the town are built on top of the aquifer that they used for drinking water. Aquifers can and sometimes absolutely do get wrecked by floods— there's even a specialized term for caves created by an aquifer collapsing away— they call it a karst. And between the mining on one side of town, the aquifers, the wells... the floodwaters might have done just that when they drained out. The valley hasn't had a full geological survey since the draining, so there's no way to know for sure, but—"

"Half the valley might be ready to just completely collapse in on itself?" He nodded. "Great." I finished the rest of the tale, up until the water hit me, I figured I could spare him the details of my own drowning at least, or let his brain fill in the gaps for me. "And then I woke up, coughing and drowning and soaked. And we're here."

Cas nodded again, clearly thinking through what to

say.

"What, too much? Too Amityville?"

He smirked before replying. "I was more thinking Carpenter. *The Fog*? All the vengeful spirits?"

"Didn't know you were a fan of the classics."

"I grew up on Rez TV. Nothing but reruns and late-night film hosts. Only the finest." We both laughed, which in my case at least was much needed. All of it had been so *strange* that now was like being awake from some sort of nightmare. At least, until I looked back in the tent at that pile of discarded wet clothing again. Cas got serious again after a moment. "All right, so, what do we have, then? I'd spout off some dreamwalk mumbo jumbo, but really you'd want my uncles for that. I'm more earth sciences and forestry preservation."

"Assuming you believe me, and you're not waiting until my back's turned to taze me and haul me off to the funny farm?"

"Oh, no. I believe you. I've seen enough weird shadows and shit on the outskirts of the valley to not believe. And that doesn't even include the whole water in your tent thing."

"OK, assuming I'm not hallucinating everything, then what we have still isn't all that much. Ghosts are real, and somehow the valley hung on to all the people who've died here. Wallace is doing something that got set up here almost a century ago. Wallace isn't even fucking Wallace, because what kind of human being drives for two days straight, goes for a big hike right afterward, takes a bullet that'd put down anyone else and just stands back up?!" I could feel my voice pitch going off. I needed to keep it together better. I took a deep breath. "All right, so I asked you to look into the Church. What did you find?" Cas grabbed a nylon sports bag from the far side of the fire, pulled out a notepad, and moved over to sit next to me.

"Not as much as I would have liked," Cas began. "The Church of Renewed Light was pretty much unique to Saltbrook. No online records, nothing to indicate it survived the flood, and nothing in written records that I could get my hands on in the last two days that wasn't connected directly to Saltbrook already. It was founded in 1863, same year the first settlements in the valley declared themselves a township by one Peter Fowler. Now, I didn't find anything on the Church before 1863, but I did find one reference to Fowler."

"Let me guess, penny dreadfuls that claimed he ate babies?"

"Close. Excommunication list from an English Methodist church up near Dover. Only reason I found it was because Oxford's digitizing all sorts of historical documents and indexing them online these days, but if it's the same Fowler, he was a Methodist priest that got kicked out about three years earlier. Must have spent the time in between immigrating and moving west."

"Ok, that's a little interesting at least. Do we know why he got the boot?"

"Nope. It's just a list of names. Then again, the Methodists still considered brawling, selling booze, and excessive swearing excommunicable offenses at that point, so it may have been nothing special."

"'Excommunicable'? Talk about your three-dollar words there, college boy."

"Yeah, I'm the terror of Scrabble Night at the watch station. Moving on from the founding stuff, there isn't much about the church itself, like I said, largely because it was so much a part of everyone's lives here. If you weren't a member, you weren't really part of the community in Saltbrook."

"Great, the real members-only club."

"Yup. And people could and were kicked out for not holding up to standards. Not that they kept a list where I could find it, but pretty much anyone who found themselves in deep shit with the church also ended up on criminal charges one way or another in town. And since Washington didn't become a state until almost twenty years after the town got founded, they held more to the opinion that local law and punishment took precedent. And it was a lot harsher than state rules, even back then. The lists of criminals? Aren't jail lists. They're hangman reports. The gallows were set up on the southwestern edge of town— first a tree, then a more formal platform."

"And they kept enforcing that right up until the flood, from what I saw in the jail. Great. Real tolerant place. I should buy a house."

Cas laughed at that one, then got more serious. "Yeah. I think it, um, might also be why those ghosts reacted to you like they did once they could see you. At least, I think holding onto the necklace let them see you, made you more real to them somehow. But this was a sundown town before they ever made up the term."

"So, they don't just hate me for being alive. They hate me for being alive *and* black at the same time. Nice to know I'm being appreciated." Looking through all the gun parts still in my lap, everything had appeared to have finished air-drying at this point, so I started reassembling the Glock, then paused. "Wait, churches and towns like this like to hate on women just as much as on us. How'd Theresa wind up in charge of the Church?"

"Inheritance. They handed down the role of priest or leader at least through the Fowler family, and by the time Theresa wound up the heir, she was also the only one left. Fun part is that she'd already married the Mayor at that point, too. Augustus Morgan."

"So, Theresa consolidated all the power in town into her own hands. Most powerful woman in the place at the end, and she was only in her thirties. Wow."

"On top of being a racist fanatical bitch who ruled the place like it was her personal queendom, yeah. Probably the only reason the state got everyone to start moving out for the flooding and the dam was because they paid so much, and because they went to all the landholders individually, instead of giving her the chance to speak for everyone or to scare them all into toeing the line."

"Which would have had the town holding a vote without her control, which is what the prayer meeting I fell into in the first place was all about. Ok, at least some of it loops back together. Do we have anything on what the stuff under Town Hall was, though?" Gun reassembled, I checked the shoulder holster and hip holster I'd hung to dry. Both still damp. Damnit. At least my climbing harness had dried out already, so I started buckling that back on.

"No idea, but the Church paid for it at least. Found that in one of the old financial records we had from the town. For the fifty-year commemoration festival, the church helped cover building expenses, renovations, and expanses for a few businesses about a year before that. If I was going to put in a secret underground anything, that's when I'd do it."

"Who all did they pay for that? Maybe there's something we can use there." Harness secured, I checked the boots— still damp as hell. The odds of those drying before I had to leave was going to be slim at best, but I left them up, just to see if they'd get a bit better.

"OK, that info I actually have." Cas paged through the notepad, into what looked like photocopied pages he'd stuck in there. "Let's see. Town Hall, the plaza and commemorative well fund (though near as I can tell, everyone contributed to that one), Cutter and Sowe— a general store that faced onto the plaza, the school, one of the foundries, and... yeah, no, that's all of them."

"So, assume something built under each of them, and, wait, where was the foundry?"

"The foundry? The west side of town, over near the mine entrances. That way ore could just be hauled straight in quicker to refine and then move out of town. It's probably just where they made the parts for whatever it was they built, though it was the biggest one of the payouts." I stopped. Construction, even then, cost a lot. More than the materials would.

"How much more did the foundry get over the others?"

"Ten thousand, but it's really not—"

"Cas, you're thinking in values now. Back then, ten grand would have bought this entire valley. That's an insane amount of money if it was just parts, even if they were huge. Which foundry was it?"

"Dubrovsky. Which was the smallest one of the lot. I remember seeing those records. Lots of brass and bronze stuff, and more casting items for sale in town rather than raw ingots to get sold out of town."

"Theresa mentioned that name, too. Something about not trusting 'him,' whatever that means. Makes sense, I guess." Then a thought occurred to me—"Did they do bells?"

"No idea. Bells?"

"Just something that kept going around. Theresa kept mentioning 'when the Lord sounds his bell' among other things. I thought with Christians it was all about trumpets for the end times. Sounded a bit off."

"Well, there's nothing either way about it."

"All right. Well, it'll have to be the foundry

anyways, that'll be the first stop once stuff dries out enough to go back in."

That last part made Cas stand up. "Alicia, I think you missed something. Look up." I did— I'd noticed and put it out of my head when I got out of the tent. The midmorning sky was darkening up with increasing cloud cover. Thick, fat rain clouds, filling up the eastern half of the horizon and pressing closer. "We've got our first storm in months coming in, and it's going to hit this afternoon or tonight. And after two months without any rain in the valley, this is going to be a downpour— practically the same as the storms that helped the floods sink the town in the first place— you're going to have flash floods, even more potential cave-ins, and all sorts of wet hazards. You need to pack it up and come back out of the valley, not go back in again. Not if you want to survive this."

Fuck. He was right about needing to hurry at least. "Cas, if I leave now, Wallace isn't going to stop because of a little rain. I have to bring him and those keys in." Neither holster had managed to dry out, the leather on both feeling more like a fully soaked sponge. I ducked into the tent and pulled my shoulder rig, still dry from the backpack out, slipped the Glock in there and then put the rig on, suppressing a grimace at the slightly awkward fit, since it had been custom shaped for the Smith and Wesson 500. Wallace was, so help me, going to pay for the loss of that gun. Hopefully it was just lying on the church floor near where I'd fallen.

"Why do I get the feeling that if I try to actually stop you, you're going to hurt me?" Cas asked, moving a step back from me.

"Wrong kind of movie, Cas. I'm not being the heroine in an action movie, I'm being the stupid bounty hunter in over her head in something very likely to kill me and anyone along for the ride." I took a step towards him and made sure he was looking directly into my eyes. "I wouldn't hurt you. I would, however, radio Charlie and tell him exactly where to come down here so he could untie you and get your underwear off your head before the valley starts flooding again." he laughed, thankfully breaking the damn mood, which is what I'd been hoping for. "Or, better yet, you can pack up this site, take my pack and stay here on the valley floor where I'll hopefully be able to radio you. Might need a hand when it comes time to get out, or more information from what all you know if something else comes up. Or I might just need a friendly voice when everything gets haunted as shit again."

"That I can do."

"Thank you." I ducked back into the tent and opened up my pack for the other gear I'd be taking. Flashlight went back onto the belt, along with my knife and the one full canteen of water I had left to me. So did the pouch holding the extra clip for the Glock, though I took out the speedloaders for the 500 and left them in the backpack. The radio Cas had originally given me still had three-quarters of battery life left to it, and I clipped that onto the belt as well. The heavy climbing gear, along with everything else, was simply going to have to stay behind. I needed to move quickly, not get snagged on a dozen things on my way through what was going to be some serious off-trail hiking. I did snag the remaining protein bars out of the pack, though, munching on one as I came back out of the tent for the last time. As I did, I could see Cas had another copy of his map spread out.

"All right," he began. "If you go in the same way as before and head straight for the plaza, then turn left on—"

"I'm not going through the town again." I interrupted. "I'll cut west, through the forest, come up at it from the south after I cross over the streambed." Cas opened his mouth to protest but I cut him off before he could get a word in. "I know, risky. But I don't want to run into Wallace again before I get more of an idea of what and why he's doing what he's doing, and going through the town practically guarantees that. And so help me, you couldn't pay me enough to go through that fucking tunnel again on the way in." I sat down and took my boots off the sticks in front of the fire. Dry socks into warm, damp boots. If there was a worst possible experience I had to list for this whole trip, this might just be near the top of the list.

Cas threw his hands up, "Why does this feel more and more like assisted suicide than a hiking trip? All right. Just keep in mind that once you get off the trail, you're in unexplored territory. No idea what you'll be dealing with going that route."

"Well, what have you guys seen from the watch station?"

"The same things we see in the rest of the valley. Trees. And a few clearings. Oh, and a giant mountain with a big bat-winged demon on it raising the dead, but we don't talk about that." We both laughed for a moment, but then an awkward silence crept in on both of us. Neither one of us wanted to talk about it, but we were both looking directly at the odds of coming out of what I'd already done alive, and here I was going back in for round two. I finally broke it by pulling the radio off my belt and thumbing it on.

"Comm check, over." Cas's radio, of course, crackled to life simultaneously.

"Yep, radio works." he replied. "All right, go get 'em." I took one last hand-check of the gear I'd strapped on, then turned and without a look back got back on the trail northwards towards the town.

8. Re-Entry

I set off at a walk up the trail that quickly turned into more of a fast lope just short of a jogging pace. Fast enough to get over the uneven trail quickly without tiring myself out too badly. After all, for this stage at least, I knew where I was headed and had an idea of the terrain. More importantly, I didn't have to take time keeping an eye on a trail or cues on the ground.

All too quickly I found myself at the first stop I wanted to make, and deliberately had avoided telling Cas about— that first mostly-intact house in the woods along the trail, stairs still caved in with the remains of that poor previous explorer at the bottom. I stood at the edge of that hole into the basement for a good minute, building up the nerve for my own little experiment, and then I thrust my hand into the pocket that contained nothing but the still-cold metal of Theresa's necklace. I could feel the shift the moment my finger touched it — as if the shadows around the edges of my vision had pulled in closer, as if everything was suddenly a touch colder, as if the forest around me was suddenly leaning in and staring at me from all sides. But the remains in that basement were unchanged. No flickering presence overlaid those bones, no ghost of a former hiker haunted this spot.

Maybe the death had been too sudden and surprising. Or maybe the valley only held on to those who'd died here long ago in the flood. Or maybe I really was going crazy and seeing things that weren't there. Who knows, but at least this one wasn't stuck here in torment, and at least I had some guarantee that if I ended up dying in all this that there was a chance I wouldn't be trapped here forever as well. That was almost reassuring.

I took my hand out of my pocket, letting the sensations that came with the necklace fade away into nothing, and pressed forward. Soon enough, I was back at that entrance to the 'Root Tunnel', staring upwards at the white hare graffiti all over again. As if this whole thing wasn't strange enough on its own without a sense of deja vu on top of it all.

I pulled out the radio and hit the broadcast switch.

"So, Cas, I'm staring at this white rabbit artwork…"

"Oh, you like that sort of thing, do you?"

"It's… not bad."

He laughed in response. "Not bad?"

"Okay, it's actually pretty good. Really good." I tracked back a little from the tunnel entrance, trying to spot a way to turn left and head through the thick layers of overgrowth instead. "But I thought you said you'd never been into town."

"Hey now. That's not the kind of thing I wanted to admit when I was trying to keep you out of it. Besides, the other side of the tunnel is literally as far as I ever went. You could feel the place not wanting visitors. Still can from here even. Going over that tunnel was as far as I ever wanted to try."

I nearly dropped the radio. "Hang on. You went *over* it?! I could've just climbed that fucking thing?"

There. There was a single-story brick building right before the buildings that formed the sides and overhang of the tunnel that had been swallowed by the overgrowth. Newer trees had even shoved their way in at places on the front wall, making the entire front wall bulge outward like someone had squeezed and pulled up a handful of dough. But the door, aside from a branch that grew up across the lower third of it was a simple set of wooden slats, already broken, twisted, and pushed in slightly from where the frame had buckled around it. I leaned back, aiming a kick up towards the center of the door, as high as I could manage. The board cracked slightly on the first kick, and the entire door shifted a bit, dropping a touch as if I'd loosened it. A second kick and the entire thing collapsed inwards, crumbling in pieces as it fell. The overcast sky and overgrown windows kept any light from penetrating— past the first square foot or so of floor covered the remains of the door, I was looking into yet another blank void from out here.

"OK, I think I've got a way around the tunnel. Going through the building right next to it— see if there's a back door or window I can squeeze through. And you better have an explanation for this 'went over' bullshit about the tunnel."

"Good luck." He paused, then resumed. "So, the left side of the tunnel where it almost touches the ground? I climbed up that and went across the top. I didn't recommend it because the ground shifted on me a couple of times when I was coming back across to leave. Didn't want to send you on a route that would've probably collapsed."

"Ok, fair. Now, going silent until I get through. I need this thing out of my hand, just in case."

"There's a hands-free switch on the bottom edge." I turned over the radio in my hands and saw it. Flicked it on. The walkie would now just do continuous two-way broadcast. Hard on the battery, but we were going to be quick, hopefully. I clipped it onto my belt.

"So there is. Thanks." I pulled out my flashlight, clicked it on, and stepped over the branch, just inside the threshold, giving my eyes a moment to adjust. I could see the general shape of the inside — one big open floorplan room, maybe ten feet by twenty, with a little bit of gray light peeping through the cracks in a dust-coated shuttered window on the far side of the room. The thick, dusty musty smell of old spaces filled my nostrils. A partial staircase to my left went up to a door that presumably let out on the roof, and another door in the back wall looked to lead out just where I needed to go. And then I looked down. Fuck. About four feet away from my boots, the floor ended, splintered away, with only some of the support beams left behind. And below that, was a sheer drop of twenty feet onto sloped limestone that wetly reflected back my flashlight, running in a sharp downwards grade from here towards town.

"Well, that confirms it. There *is* a... what did you call it? Cave running under the town. The edge of it comes up right under here."

"It's called a karst. How deep does it go?"

"No idea, it slopes down pretty quick from here,

though. Certainly don't want to go falling down it."
Oh, this was going to be a *stupid* idea, but I didn't
see any other way to do it. The support beams left
from the floor looked solid enough, and more than
enough of them ran from here over to that back
door. It'd be a short walk across the one main beam,
and then just crossing over to the one that ran
perpendicular to it that was just a foot away from
the far wall and the door. I carefully stretched out
one leg, slowly putting my boot onto the beam and
leaning into it carefully add my weight. The wood
creaked, but not alarmingly so. I brought my other
foot off the floor and settled my full weight onto the
beam. No shifting, no further creaks. OK, I could do
this. The beams themselves were a good ten inches
wide. *Nice solid old-world construction*, I laughed to
myself.

Slowly, carefully, I walked out towards the far side
of the room. Two feet. Four feet. Six. Eight. The
board held, solid as a rock, and I reached the point
where it transitioned onto the beam that ran the
length of the building. I could even reach up a
hand to steady myself on the wall if I wanted as
I went. Not that I did, but still. All right. Roughly
sixteen feet to cross to get in front of the door. I
could do this. Fourteen. Twelve. I noticed as I went,
that with going in this direction, I was moving
roughly in the direction that the karst floor below
me sloped downwards, which meant the drop got

significantly greater with each step that I took. I swallowed back a gulp. Eight more feet. Four more. I realized I was holding my breath and slowly exhaled. Two more feet. There. I was positioned right in front of it. No lock of any kind of the door itself, just a turn-knob to push it outward, which grudgingly gave way in my hand, like something was gripping it on the far side, and stepping with one foot onto the two bare feet of flooring in front of the door, I pushed.

Nothing. I might as well have been pushing against the brick wall. I tried again, shoving into it with a shoulder, the door shaking a little in its frame, and stopped when I realized dirt was beginning to pour in around the edges and top of the doorframe. Fuck. The window might have been clear, but the door itself must've been drifted in with sediment from the lake on the other side. I wasn't getting out this way. I turned around on the narrow ledge. I'd have to go back, but the beam didn't just run back to that junction. If I walked all the way back across and didn't turn, I'd be right under the broken remains of the stairs that led to the roof. If I was going to get through from this building, I'd have to at least try.

I gingerly stepped out onto the beam again, trying to carefully keep my focus on the wood, and not on the sheer drop below me that at this point had the bottom out of the reach of my flashlight's beam. Step by slow step, I crossed back over that emptiness again, slowly seeing the cave floor rise to meet me, and still stopping far enough below me to be a deadly fall at best. I made it back to the junction unharmed and stepped cautiously over it to continue towards the stairs. Four steps to get me under the stairs. On the first one, I could hear the board creak under me again— not alarmingly so, but enough to worry. The second step, nothing. On the third, I could see it— the point where the end of this beam met the wall of the building would normally be a slot in the brick wall, with the beam fully supported by layers of bricks underneath, extending down to the basement floor. Only here, there was a single brick left under the board, and the rest of the wall had collapsed away into the karst below. And what had caught my gaze wasn't the brick itself, but the minute fall of dust as the mortar around the brick continued to crumble and fall away, as it had probably been doing with each vibration of the board.

I looked up at the stairs. The stairway had broken off about three feet above where the floor would have been, making it almost three and a half feet above where I was. If I was going to jump and grab onto it, I needed to be closer— I'd barely make the jump from here. There was only going to be one way to do this, and that brick was sure to go with my next step no matter which way I went. I reached down, trying to keep my movements as small as possible, shake the beam as little as I could, and clipped my flashlight back onto my belt. Didn't want to risk losing it on the jump. I took one deep breath. Another. And on the third I took one hard fast step forward, getting as much momentum as I could and putting it into a mad leap for the stairs, trying to get onto them and distribute as much of my weight across them as I could. The beam pitched under me, falling and sliding diagonally at first as it pulled free from one side then the other, then tumbling away into the darkness below. I hung in the air for a moment, suspended in the dim light of the room, not able to see well enough with my light hanging downwards to tell if I was even going to hit the steps, or just sail uselessly underneath them into the wall. And then I hit, the bottom edge of the staircase slamming into me just below my ribs. My outstretched arms scrabbled for a grip on the steps above me as my weight started to slide back into the hole under me, and then my hand caught the far side of one of the steps where the vertical strip of wood above it had already broken away. I got my other hand back up near it and pulled forward, dragging my hip, and then my knees up onto the bottom of the steps. The wood was creaky but it held, and I cautiously stood up and walked up the few remaining ones between me and the door. The metal here had rusted away ages ago, the wood of the door itself only held upright by a thin scrim of dust and sediment at the base. One push and the entire thing fell outwards onto the roof of the building, and I stepped out blinking into the heavily overcast daylight.

The roof was flat, painted wood that had been stripped down by everything that happened to the valley, so I worked my way cautiously around the edge, not trusting any of it to hold any better than what had been inside. And on the west side of the building, as I'd guessed, a slope of earth ran up the side, gaping around the window a bit, but otherwise solid and almost reaching up to the roof itself. Looking past that, I could see out a bit further into the valley from this height, though not as far as I'd hoped— a single story of height doesn't make a lot of difference when you're dealing with hundred-foot tall fir and pine trees, which were what extended from here clear out as far as I could see. There was a break in the trees ahead of me though, not a path or a game trail, just a normal organic space between trees big enough for me to get through, so I set off down the slope towards it.

"Okay…" came Cas's voice over the radio. "That was a lot of crashing. Everything ok?"

I'd forgotten he'd been picking up every loud noise that had happened while I was in there. "I'm all right— just clearing another hurdle. I'm past the building, and moving west back into the woods now."

The hole in between the trees was short enough I had to duck to get in at first, but past that first row of trees were a number of older taller ones— the forest must have just been slowly encroaching on the back of the building still. I was able to make my way forwards. The ground through here was shot through with the roots of both the currently living and older petrified trees, making for a bumpy, uneven walk, like stumbling and rolling across a heaving ship's deck. Between the jumps and impacts inside and trying to maintain a pace over this ground, I could feel the soreness already starting in my legs. If everything was like this between here and the foundry, I was going to be exhausted by the time I got that far.

After what was maybe ten minutes of stumbling through the forest, though, the trees ended almost as suddenly as they'd begun, leaving me stumbling out onto bare dirt and rock, probably the first stretch of bare earth this big I'd seen since coming down into the valley. Looking up from my feet, I could see it extended in a wide curve a good twenty feet wide, stretching away to both the northeast and southwest. Ahead of me, there was also a sudden dip in the ground that ran through the center of this barren patch, and I walked up to it cautiously. It was more than a dip, to be honest — this was more like someone had dug a canal, only they'd reversed the measurements— while the line that had been cut was maybe two feet at its widest here, it ran deep— nearly six feet straight down. I took out my flashlight again and shined it into the hole, and was surprised when I saw something had stained the currently dry ground at the bottom with bright red, blue, and gold metallics that swirled around each other in rippling waves of intense color.

"Hey, Cas, I think I've found the infamous brook, though it's gone dry right now. That and someone painted the thing." I went on to describe what I was seeing.

"That's not paint," Cas replied. "It's staining from runoff from both the mines and the mountain streams that fed into here. Iron, copper, tin, and a few other things."

"What's the gold part of all the colors?"

"Pyrite. Iron sulfide, though there's probably deposits of straight-up sulfur that fed into there as well. The creek was toxic as hell, even before settlers started out here, not that it stopped them from drinking and doing everything else in it at first."

"Oof. That couldn't have done much good for the local populace." I took the momentary pause to stretch— the treeline on the far side of the creek looked better than what I'd just crossed, but not by much.

"It didn't. Lot of low birthrates at first. Go figure. Of course, our good friends at the Church of Renewed Light didn't let a silly thing like literal poison stop them from holding baptisms in it."

"Seriously?"

"Seriously. They played the 'the valley is our Eden' shtick to the hilt. I'm looking at a photo from your file here of Theresa baptizing someone right now. Must've been a few years before they put in the dams, but they just kept right on with it."

"Ugh. And quit looking through the photos and finish packing up my camp, will you? I want to be ready to run out of here once we're done."

"It's already mostly done. Just taking a breather while we're talking. What's up ahead should just be just forest. I don't have a lot of information on it, but if you just stick to a northwest bearing, you'll hit the foundries, or if you cut a bit further east, the mine entrance, and then just backtrack from there."

"Got it. Just me and what, five miles of spooky-ass probably haunted woods?"

"Pretty close. Radios should be good for ten miles, so you should have me with you the whole way."

"Great. Let's do this, then." And with that, I stepped

across the creek bed. Rest break done with. Time to head back in.

9. History Lessons

"...OK, so is there a *Mister* Lake back home, or?"

Cas's question damn near had me tripping and falling full on my face for the roots I was navigating over at the time.

"What the fuck?" I replied. "Did we hit 'awkwardly personal questions' hour and nobody bothered to tell me?"

"You've been silent for like fifteen minutes. I needed something to break the anxiety. That or I was gonna start assuming you were horribly devoured by ghosts."

"Did you really want a running commentary of 'Oh, look, it's a tree. And another tree. And YET

ANOTHER tree.' the whole time?" To be fair, the landscape had changed up a little bit since crossing the creekbed. Over the last leg of this hike, I'd seen a slow shift from pines interspersed with even more petrified pines to more deciduous trees— oaks and maples, with fewer intact petrified trees and more broken ones littering the ground instead. I guess the bulkier trunks that didn't work like straight vertical columns didn't hold their own weight as well. There were also occasional patches of apple trees that had gone wild, which left me wondering if I'd started stumbling through what had been someone's orchard originally. While there was more space between the trunks, the ground itself was still such a tumult of new and far older roots, rock, and moss that it was still more bouldering or climbing than what could be considered a walk. My legs burned with strain at this point, and I took the opportunity to stop and stretch for a moment while I responded to Cas, leaning up against the broken stump of a petrified tree.

"All right." I said. "For the record, there is no Mister Lake. Or Missus. Not for lack of trying on anyone's part, either, I'm just not wired that way. Like, at all." All right. One leg up onto the stump, bending forwards over it, feeling the pull from Achilles tendon all the way up into the hamstring.

"So, aromantic or asexual?" Cas inquired.

"Both, really. Don't want to get attached, and don't like the idea of it. And before it gets said— experimented more than enough to prove I was just never into it." Now the other leg. Feel the pull, let the muscle relax into it, and ease off some of that urge to cramp up.

"Hunh. I never would have —" I cut him off before he could get any farther.

"If I have to hear another 'never figured a Black girl wouldn't be into sex' comment, I'm turning this thing off and making you hike out alone." Stretching done, I set off again, going directly over the stump, and working my way through another pair of trees.

"Retracted. Sorry— should've known better in the first place. Heard more than enough shit about Natives to last a life already."

"Apology accepted. So, enough with making me uncomfortable. How long have you and Charlie been a thing?"

"I… we haven't… but…" came the spluttering over the radio, and I held back a laugh. "Damnit, Alicia, he's *straight*. Or at least still thinks he is. And how did you know?"

I didn't bother keeping the laugh to myself this time, and let it out. "Being a private detective is good for a few things. That and learning how to pick up on body language cues. If you're worried about it, don't be, it's not anything that shows all that heavily."

"You know saying that is going to make me worry even *more*, right? Where did you even learn learn all that? Detective school?"

"College, mostly. Bits in the psych and sociology courses. The private detective courses on offer in New York are decent, but they don't cover everything." The trees just kept coming, with little to no variation, but ahead and to the left, I thought I could see more sunlight filtering through the branches, so I adjusted a bit in that direction.

"College girl. Nice. So were you planning on being a private eye from the beginning?"

"Yeah. Took a bachelor's in criminal justice, but this was always the plan. Growing up in foster care, you learn early on not to have much trust for cops or any other agency out there."

"So, why law enforcement at all?"

"Not law enforcement. Helping people. I could give a fuck about most of the shit cops are after. And most of the bounty jobs I take are for people the cops are too lazy to go after. Or ones for people too privileged one way or another for most cops to want to bother touching." It *was* a break in the trees. I pushed further left, and there, I could see it— an open stretch of land. My legs needed it too badly. I got up to the edge of the treeline to take a careful look.

"So, what, you decided to go full Robin Hood? Punish the powerful, save the poor?"

I snorted. "I'm no vigilante. I take jobs for people, and hunt bounties in between." Looking across, it looked like just an open field, maybe a quarter-mile across— no trees, just long tall grass gone to seed, a bit over waist-high, browned from the dry summer months, with some kind of structure towards the north end of the field— I couldn't tell the details well enough from here. But no signs of houses, walls, or buried foundations that would leave to more caving in basements, which was what I was worried about at the time. My legs needed some regular flat terrain for a bit and this was perfect.

"See? Hero for Hire. The whole Lu—" I cut him off right there.

"Do not give me the Luke Cage speech. He didn't charge a per diem or expenses, and I do. Now give me a minute here." I stepped out into the grass. Letting myself take it slow across what had suddenly turned into a much smoother walk. While the clouds overhead had thickened and darkened more and more, there were still occasional gaps where midafternoon sun filtered through, and one of those few golden rays shone down on the field. I stretched out in the warm glow for a moment, luxuriating in the chance to move a little more freely. Then it struck me. "Cas, you said it was forest all the way through from the creek to the mines, right? I'm standing in a wide open field. It's small, so it might not have been spotted from the watch station, but what is this place?"

"Like I said before, there's some natural clearings and stuff."

"No, Cas." I kept walking, working back up to full speed, feeling the tension of all the tripping and stumbling over roots fading down to just the slow burn of lots and lots of walking. "This is a *field*. Man-made. It still even has mostly rectangular sides, though it might not look like it from the station. About two, two and a half miles, so somewhere right in between the creekbed and the mines? Did anything used to be here?" I rubbed my arms as I kept walking. It was somehow colder out here, even in the sun, but I didn't pay it much attention as I walked, gabbing the canteen off my belt to take a few sips of water.

"Keep moving, Alicia, I want to check the maps and those notes you gave me." Cas sounded distracted, then again, he was probably already digging through the papers. I put the canteen back and shivered, wrapping my arms around myself. It definitely felt colder. I felt like I should be freezing, though there weren't any signs of sudden cold around me— no frost, my breath didn't even steam in the air. I could see the structure at the north end of the field more clearly now as well. It was a tree, or what remained of one. Petrified like all the older living trees during the flood, only this was an oak, not a pine or fir. Twisted and huge, the massive trunk broken off only ten or twelve feet above the ground, branches long gone, and stained black by whatever had stained it during the saponification process. What had made me think it was a structure was all the debris piled up against it in an irregular hump— boards and pilings tumbled together in a jumble, the wood gone the bleached grey of driftwood from its own long soak in the floodwater.

The cold feeling I had seemed *thicker* somehow. Like it was resisting me walking through it. I took one more halting step forward, then another. I could feel my own pulse pounding in my ears, drowning out Cas saying something incomprehensible on the radio, and yet I couldn't take my eyes off that tree at the end of the field. At the same time, there was another, sharper cold presence— the necklace in my pocket— it was always cold, but now it was so cold it felt like my thigh muscles were going to cramp up where it rested in my pocket. It was almost a reflex, reaching down to get the source of the cold away from my leg before it could hurt me. Cas was yelling something I couldn't hear over the radio. I was shivering. My fingertip touched the silver of the necklace.

In a heartbeat, everything shifted. This wasn't the gradual shift from the fall before, but as sudden and abrupt as someone turning off a light switch. The sky went out, turning into blackness streaked and covered by grey and white clouds that somehow left just enough illumination to see. The trees bordering the field had become twisted imitations of themselves, leafless, stripped, and lifeless black needles jutting upwards at the sky. I turned around in a slow circle, taking everything in. The field itself had lost all semblance of life, grasses withering away to expose dry earth in an instant. Bumps and mounds hidden by the grasses were exposed, though, and I could see details that must not have existed in reality, because I would have tripped over them coming through. The rounded hollowed bumps where the dirt covered skulls in only a thin layer. Long stretching bumps of arms and legs. Curves of ribs, spines, and pelvises, all barely covered by lifeless earth. And so many of them. I must have walked past dozens, if not hundreds already.

I was walking through a mass grave. A huge one. Decades of Saltbrook's victims lay in the earth all around me. More disturbing was the total lack of ghosts. I'd been seeing spirits all over the valley, but here, at what was probably the largest collection of bodies in the entire county, there was nothing. Then again, maybe it was good that these spirits had moved on. They'd suffered enough in life, being trapped here would only have been more torment for them, I'm sure.

And then, I heard the creaking behind me and turned back around again to see it in full. The oak tree from the end of the field now *towered* over that end of the open space, well over fifty feet high, branches reaching out like clutching hands and fingers. Shadows moved and roiled across the bark like oil on the surface of a puddle, coiling back on themselves like serpents rearing up to strike. And on every single branch, in some cases multiple swinging from the same branch, were the nooses, all of them empty, waiting and twitching like hungry claws waiting for the right moment to strike. Swinging back and forth slightly to create the noise I'd heard, even though there was no wind at the moment. Stained and blackened with age long before the floodwaters had darkened them further and destroyed them. Somehow the gallows tree had taken on a life of its own, enough to leave its own hungry ghost here where I could see it. This was definitely not something that had ever been human. Somehow I had a feel of the nature of the thing, like all the hatred of those who had persecuted all the people buried around me had settled and pooled here with every last drop of justified anger and fury of those who'd been hung until it all turned in on itself, festering, hostile, and *hungry*.

I ran. I am not ashamed to admit my first gut reaction to all of this at this point was one born straight out of fear. Giant ghostly hangman's tree spells RUN in just about any book as far as I'm concerned. I had enough presence of mind to turn eastward, so I was still traveling in a direction more towards the mines and the foundries than back out of here, but I was not about to get any closer to that tree if I could fucking help it, and I ran. As my hand left my pocket, the imagery around me began to fade almost immediately, reality reasserting itself over everything as I tore across the empty field.

"Alicia! Alicia! Are you there?" Cas was nearly yelling into the goddamn radio, but I didn't bother replying, saving my breath for the run until I was through the trees on the northeast corner of the field and a good fifty feet inside the forest again. I finally stopped, lungs clawing for air while my legs burned from strain, slumping back against a tree into a half-crouch.

I pulled the radio out in front of me, not sure of my voice at this point, and also just needing to have actual physical contact with something at this point. "I'm here." I paused for another deep breath or two. "Fuck. Yeah, I'm here. I'm ok."

"What happened?" he asked, and I related it quickly, in between gasps of air as I cooled down from the sprint. I realized one thing as I was talking it all out, though, and brought it up at the end. "It didn't chase me."

"What?"

"The tree. It didn't chase me, or come after me, or even move really." I pushed myself back up to standing, and started moving forwards again, roughly reorienting myself as best as I could. "It was like it was waiting for something."

"Waiting for what?"

"I don't know. I'm more worried that I'm going to find out."

10. Foundry

Over an hour of picking my way through the thick forest north of the field later, swapping stories with Cas over the radio to keep my own sanity, him talking about growing up on the Colville reservation but having to bus in to the mostly white town of Colville for school, me talking about growing up in (again, mostly white) foster care in upstate New York. I was so worn out that when I stumbled out of the trees onto open land and saw the giant skull, I nearly fell over laughing from exhaustion, instead of feeling any dread or fear. As it was, though, I was silent, more from the bone-deep weariness that was starting to set in after all the uneven terrain.

To be fair, that is what the entrance to mines looked

like from this angle— a side view of a skull, shaped from the debris of the mine and outlying buildings that had been broken apart by the flood and shoved into the hillside where the entrance was. You could see the rounded curve of the side and back of the head there, the suggestion of an eye socket in the way a dark outcropping of rock jutted above the open yawn of the mouth that was the entrance to the mine itself, all shaped out of randomly drifted wood, logs, metal pilings, and even a few whole stripped trees. I stared at it for a moment, knowing it had to be a trick of the eye, before I circled around towards the front. As I moved, the rest of the pile-up of debris resolved itself more into random chaos than anything resembling a shape, except for the open hole that was left of the mine entrance, which still yawned open like a broken-toothed maw. There was even a cobblestone road, largely caked over with dirt, that went right down its throat in one direction, and extended back into town in the other.

"Cas, I'm here." It took me a moment to realize I needed to clarify. "I'm at the mine entrance. Where to now?"

"Right, let me see." I could hear him turning through pages, presumably going for the map and the notes he'd put together. "OK, turn back towards the town and head that way— due east. Mining company buildings were on the south side, independents on the north, so it should be the third building on your left. May have to go a ways to get to it."

"Third on my left, got it." No rest for the wicked. I set off, taking my time on the downhill path towards town. At first, all the buildings I could see were on my right, most of them big warehouse foundations that had been completely obliterated by the flood. From what I'd understood, they'd been standing empty and already abandoned before that anyways, the mines having been shut down as nonprofitable even before the decision to flood the valley. Still, it was nice to see nothing more creepy than a few abandoned lots and crumbling piles of bricks where walls had once met at corners. The forest was only just beginning to encroach on these spaces, the land in this area having been cleared out both for lumber and to give much needed space back in the time before the flood. New trees were still just working their way in at the edges of things, with the occasional upshoot coming up through the cracks. I had to circle around one such pine tree that must have managed to find purchase right in the center of the road right after the flooding had receded— it was already a good thirty feet tall, with roots zigging and zagging around the cobblestones, trying to find soil to get a grip into as it grew and expanded.

Going past the tree, though, I could already see

the first of the foundries coming up on my left. Like the actual mining company buildings, this one had been built more like a large-scale warehouse, presumably to give room inside for casting work and everything else needed. However, while the roof had mostly survived the intervening years, the walls hadn't. Wooden beams and timbers had burst outwards from the building like the unfolding petals of a flower, the roof settling down to rest on the ground beneath it. Hopefully the other two were in better condition, but I didn't try to get my hopes up.

As I continued on, I noticed it was getting visibly darker by the minute. Looking up, the cloud cover had become total, with even darker clouds pushing in to cover the valley from the east. At the same time, I was coming up against the same problem that I'd hit before— the high walls of the valley meant that while the sun might still be up, it was already sinking past the valley's edge. It was going to get fully dark, and soon with the storm coming in. You could feel the shift in air pressure as it came on.

The second foundry, designed similarly to the first, hadn't fared much better. While the treeline was much closer-in here, the pressures of time and current had staved in the western half of the building, and the rest simply fell in on top of the wreckage. However, the trees had already filled in the gaps between the second and third buildings, leaving me rather surprised by what I found with the third foundry.

The sign above the wide double doors simply said "DUBROVSKY" in letters that had been carved into the wood, with a few paint-flakes of decoration still clinging to the grain in spots. The sign itself, like the front wall of the barn-like structure that was the front end of this foundry, were bowed outward, pushed into a curve by pressure from the trees, which had grown in and up so close to the building that two of them had now become the front corner supports of it. Given the overgrowth, it was hard to get a sense of the true scale of the place— smaller than the other foundries, to be sure, but it looked like at least part of it hooked into an L-shape towards the back. The only way to be sure was to get inside and see, so I walked up to the doors and gave them a try.

No luck. Between the warping and rusted fixtures, they may as well have been part of the wall, but the wood itself was rotted and damaged enough that the section of wood the handle was bolted onto started to give way and pull away from the door. I regretted leaving my climbing axe back with the rest of my gear, but at least I still had my knife. Pulling it out, I flipped open the heavy lever-lock blade, and worked the point of the knife in as far as I could, didn't want to snap off the tip, before starting to turn and push the handle upwards, forcing the board out further and further, until I could get my free hand over the top of it. I dropped the knife carefully to one side, grabbed that top edge with both hands, and pulled, the board coming free with several pops as rusted nails either broke off or pulled loose. The vertical board came fully free from the door, giving me a six-inch wide, three-foot tall hole. I started in on the top edge of the next plank over with the knife, and in about a minute of work, managed to get it free as well, giving me just barely enough room to squeeze in sideways. I put the knife away, brought out the flashlight, and pulled myself in through the hole.

Inside, the comparison to a barn sadly held up. Wide open brick floor across the entire space, another pair of double doors at the back, and next to nothing else aside from a partial loft running down the east side at the second story. The western wall was mostly gone, no doubt broken away in the floods, but the boards had largely been replaced by tree trunks growing in close enough together to form an effective barrier. Newer saplings had even started to push aside the bricks of the floor on that side of the room. Most of the roof was gone, letting in enough light to see by, so I put the flashlight back. But no tools or furniture, no plans or records, nothing was left, not even enough debris to consider garbage.

"Goddamnit. Well, I made it to the foundry, Cas."

"That doesn't sound good."

"The building's still here, but there's nothing left inside. Everything got swept away in the flood. Or cleared out before then."

"Fuck. Well, it was worth trying. What's next, heading back into the main half of town?" Cas was probably right with that idea. It was the sane, logical choice that all my experience as a bounty hunter and detective said I should be doing. But deep down, part of me knew that the answers I still needed were *here*. In this room. I just had to use the right tool to see them.

I took a deep breath. "No, I'm trying something *completely* stupid first. Now be quiet, I'll radio in a few minutes." and I reached behind me and flicked the radio off. One more deep breath, and then before I could stop myself, I thrust my hand into my pocket, grabbing the icy chunk of metal that was Theresa's necklace, pulling it out, and keeping it in my closed fist.

The foundry seemed to whirl around me in a blur of motion as time itself went through a high-speed rewind. I could see the trees that made the western wall rapidly shrink their way back into the ground, bricks shifting back into place, the hole in the wall suddenly open and free, flooding the room with that sourceless, directionless, grey ghostlight I'd seen before, and then suddenly everything was submerged once more into dark blues and greens of the floodwaters. I saw the wood of the walls suddenly regain color, shifting from the light grey into dark and swollen with water. The ceiling suddenly came back into existence, building itself out of seemingly nothing, and then the western wall timbers swept back in, knitting themselves into place like a scar covering over a wound. The blue-green light faded, leaving the ghostlight tracing out the empty interior. It was like everything hung still for a moment, though I could see shifting trails of mice or rats blur their way through the dust on the floor. And then the dust disappeared. The wood of the walls took on polish and color, and with even more blurring speed of people moving through in high-speed reverse, furniture began to appear— heavy tables appearing from nowhere and forming themselves into multiple workstations in the space, quickly becoming cluttered with carving tools, hammers, and all manner of objects. The motion became faster and faster, winding back the years before the flood, and then, just as suddenly as it had begun, it stopped.

I stood in a cluttered but organized workshop, tools and bookshelves hanging on the walls, wide tables where masters and apprentices would finish work on polishing and assembling cast items all around me. I could see flickering blurs of movement here and there. Ghostly loops of memory of people as they worked, but nothing concrete, as if whatever happened here wasn't enough to tie these particular ghosts to this place. Cautiously, I reached out a hand, trying to grab a pair of pliers casually left out on the table in front of me, only to have my hand pass directly through them and the table below them. Ok, so this would be like before, only less interaction this time around.

The back doors of the shop opened, held by flickering half-seen workers, as a heavy wooden cart pushed by four more of the ghostly flickering humanoid shapes came through the space. On top of the cart was a massive, cloth-draped item. Impossible to tell what it was, aside from the roundness, but it barely fit through the doors coming into the shop from the back. It passed through the back doors, down the cleared walkway in the center of the shop, passed right through where I was standing, obscuring everything in darkness for a brief flash, and went out the front doors.

flicker

Some of the tools shifted position. One of the worktables now blocked the aisleway. There were still the occasional flickers of ghostly workers here and there at the tables or moving through the doors, but they were slower, now, moving forwards at a normal pace in the brief flashes I could see them. And then from behind me, Theresa's voice nearly startled me into a jump. I turned to see her, ghostly pale as always, still an adult, but younger than when I'd seen her previously at the church and the town hall. She had both hands on her hips and was looking up angrily at whoever it was she was talking to.

"...no, I have told you already, we have the construction of the mechanism and the locks fully under control, and almost done already to your specifications. All I'm here for is an assurance that you'll be delivering on time. The commemoration festival is three weeks away, construction on everything else is almost done, but the well cannot be laid down until after you've delivered your part of the bargain." A moment's pause, she started nodding in reply to something, though I couldn't see what, and then she faded away just as suddenly.

flicker

The workbenches shifted, then shifted again. Tools moved about various times, first in one spot, then another, workers flitted past at high speed, and then it slowed to a normal pace crawl again. Theresa, looking similar to how she had a moment ago, maybe a bit younger, followed by two men carrying a third body, wrapped in a sheet, by the shoulders and ankles. Her voice rang out in the confines of the workshop "Dubrovsky! Where are you! I need your miracle again." Her voice cracked on that last part, the commanding tone she was used to using switching to one of desperation. "Please. It's been less than three days. It has to be soon enough. I need him." I could *feel* a presence behind me, though looking over my shoulder, I didn't see anything to indicate someone was actually there. I looked back to catch the end of Theresa nodding.

"I understand," she replied to thin air. "No guarantees. But we have to *try*. If I lose him, we could lose the whole town." Lose the town? Wait, was that her husband, Augustus, the mayor, wrapped up in that sheet? What the hell had been going on in here? She was listening to some reply I couldn't hear again, then said "We have to try it. Too many of our plans hinge on him being alive. Plans that affect you and me both. Do it." A pause, she nodded, and then Theresa, followed by the others walked through and past me, going towards the back doors of the workshop, fading away just before they reached them.

flicker

Another shift. More rapid motion. And there was Theresa, definitely younger this time, barely out of her teens, sitting slumped over one of the worktables.

"I don't *understand* why the miracle didn't work! We should have been able to save Uncle Thomas. He should have been alive again! It hadn't been that long, just as soon as I could get to him after the funeral. Why didn't it work?" She paused as if listening for an answer. "Well then," she replied. "Is there a way to *make* it more powerful?"

flicker

I heard a noise behind me and turned in time to spot her as she passed through the doors into the shop. A girl, maybe eight or nine years old, holding a small wooden box. She had a plain, but thin face— baby fat still hanging on to those cheeks stubbornly, and the reddened eyes and slightly damp nose of someone who'd been crying right up until they walked in here. I didn't recognize the waifish brown-haired child at first until I saw something I recognized around her neck— the same silver cross I held in my hand. This was what Theresa Fowler had looked like as a kid? Then again, weird fanaticism can come in all kinds of packages, I supposed. She carried the box over to one of the closer worktables, set it down, and was waiting, patiently, staring up expectantly at someone who... wasn't there. Great. I was going to only get one side of the conversation, if I was lucky.

She finally spoke, in a choked-up voice, and said "Pa-Pa," I don't know if it was a regionalism, or just her own way of talking about her dad, but she almost made it sound like 'pop pop', as two separate words. "Papa told me to ask you about your special project. He said it could help. With Mittens." and she opened up the box. Inside was a kitten, not even a year old, fur soaked and matted with water, though white socks stood out against the brown and black fur on three of its feet, clearly both drowned and dead. Poor thing.

I didn't hear any sound made in reply, but a moment later, I saw a wooden box, slightly larger than the one Mittens had been interred in, lift itself off of another table, floating bumpily through the air as if it were being carried through the space between tables back over to where Theresa waited. And as the box crossed through the central walkway, I could see one shred of evidence— there may not have been a ghost, but, unlike every other apparition here, there was a shadow in the pale ghostlight, holding onto the shadow of the box as it stretched out across the floor. Gauging how someone actually looks from a shadow from a weird light source was nearly impossible, but at a guess, I would've said male, and definitely big. At least it was something. The box came to rest on the table a few inches away from Theresa's box.

There was a brief moment of silence, and then Theresa nodded in reply to something. *Damnit, kid, talk, I can't tell shit from a nod!* I remember thinking to myself. Then the lid of the box slowly opened, and a bell was lifted out. It was a handbell, maybe a foot long in total from the mouth to the end of the hardwood shaft it had been mounted on for holding. The bell itself was bronze, shot through with thick veins of something darker, faintly redder than the rest of the greenish-gold material, instead of being rounded and flaring outward like most handbells I'd seen this was more cylindrical, yet still had four distinct sides to it that bulged slightly outward, like the bells I'd seen in pictures of Shinto temples before. There was also a raised band running around the center of all four sides— I wasn't sure if it served some purpose or was part of the decoration. And there was no clapper hanging in the middle. Instead, a wooden rod was lifted out of the box a moment later for use as a striker.

The striker hovered over the bell for a moment, then swung into action, quickly hitting one side, then another of the bell, in a few short strikes playing out a small tune. None of the sound from the bell carried over to me. All I could hear was an eerie silence, finally perforated by a tiny cough and hacking noise. I stepped closer, and there, convulsing in the box, coughing up a runny stream of water and bodily fluids, was Mittens, clearly alive once more. The kitten let out a few more coughs, then just stood there and breathed for a moment, before finally turning all-white eyes that had filmed over during the time it had spent dead up to Theresa and letting out a plaintive meow. Theresa of course, squealed with delight, picked the cat up and hugged it to herself. And then everything— Theresa and the kitten, the tables, the tools, all of it, faded away. The holes in the wall and ceiling reappeared, as did the trees, and the ghostlight guttered and died, leaving me blinking to adjust my eyes to the near-nighttime darkness that had descended on the shop.

I waited a moment, the necklace still as cold as a lump of ice in my hand, but nothing further happened. I think I'd seen everything I was going to be allowed to see that way. I put it back in my pocket. So. I was standing in a foundry that had made a bell that could bring a kitten back to life. And somehow, if I wasn't missing my guess, they managed to pull off something bigger. Far bigger. I had to see the rest. I went to the back doors— while the hinges had rusted through, they hadn't been shattered under pressure like the ones on the front doors— the right door didn't so much as open when I pulled the handle, it came completely free of the frame, and I found myself, having to shift over the whole door a few feet before propping it up against the wall and the frame. I don't know why I took such care with it, I just somehow felt that I needed to not make any big crashing noises right now, not here.

The back doors opened out onto an open courtyard, with what I'd thought of as an extension of the main building actually a whole separate building to my right. The courtyard itself was packed earth, though, with three odd structures made from brick and rusted iron— it took me a minute to recognize, but then I realized they were coal-burning crucibles, each one designed to set large amounts of ore melting all at once. Stunted trees grew in and around everything, with ivy reaching up across most of the brickwork. I remembered back to one sculptor friend in New York when I'd been in college. If they were melting the metal like this, then they needed a space to pour it, which must have been what the other barn-sized extension was for. I went over to the entrance to it, to discover that this set of doors had already been shifted open by age, currents, or whatever in the intervening year— there was a wide enough gap between them to slip through, and so I did, turning on my flashlight as I went in.

The interior was pitch-black, and I had to marvel at the fact that there was actually an intact building solid enough to block out what little light was left in the day in the area. Then as I started looking around from the doorway, I could see why— heavy iron I-beam supports braced the walls and ceiling, as well as forming overhead support for a massive pulley and winch. With all that in here, there hadn't been much room for the wood exterior to shift in the flood. Looking at the floor, though, I stopped myself before I could go much further. There was a ten-by-ten foyer area where bricks had been laid down, but past that was a floor of open sand. It had drifted some with the flood, leaving the left side down by about a foot from the right, which had spilled up over the top of the narrow walkway that ran down both sides of the sandpit. This must have been where they poured the metal for castings, using it to fill impressions left in the damp sand or to burn out wax models. In the flashlight's beam, I could pick out another section of brick flooring on the far side of the pit, with at least one overturned worktable and a number of spilled objects on the ground. If there were plans or anything, they'd be back there.

I picked my way carefully down the left-hand walkway. Given the state of everything, I didn't trust trying to walk on that sand one bit if I could help it. On reaching the back, I could see what I was looking at decently in the flashlight's beam — under layers of dust and spilled sand, where the floodwaters must have spilled them off tables or knocked them off the shelves that stood to one side, were the wooden forms— dummy shapes that would be pressed into the sand so the impressions could then be filled with liquid metal. There were doorknobs, all kinds of handles, key blanks, various statues and decorative pieces, several bells, though these looked to be of the more western design than the one I'd seen in the ghostly visions earlier. None of this seemed to be it, though. I remembered Theresa's ghost, leaning on the worktable, asking just how one could 'make it more powerful', as I played the flashlight's beam across the rough back wall.

And then I realized that I wasn't looking at a back wall. I could see the wall behind it, but between me and the wall was a huge object, bulky and wrapped in canvas that had been soaked down and hardened onto the thing in the flood, then slowly frayed open in spots over the years. I couldn't tell what was under that canvas, aside from that it was big, so I grabbed the canvas at one of the points where it frayed enough to have an edge to grip, and pulled, hard. At first, it cracked, breaking more like a layer of shellac, a six-foot long chunk of the hardened canvas just breaking free entirely of it in my grip. I tossed it aside, stuck the flashlight in my mouth and gripped it with my teeth so I still had light, and grabbed another section and half ripped, half broke it free. And another. And another. Like breaking the shell off some kind of egg. Dust filled the air, powdering out of the canvas chunks in thick clouds, and I found myself nearly choking on it. I backed away onto the walkway to give it a minute to settle and to cough out what I'd breathed in. I ended up grabbing my canteen out and using the last of the water I was carrying to wash my mouth out and get a much-needed drink.

As the dust settled and my lungs cleared, I could feel it. It sat back there, in the back of the room as a heavy, almost malevolent presence. I could feel that same creeping chill without the air actually getting any colder. It somehow knew I was here. It had just been sitting here, all this time, waiting for discovery. I finally brought the beam of the flashlight up to slowly play across the bulk of the thing.

It was massive, a curved cylinder that had been carved out of not just one, but several tree trunks, encircled by a heavy band of rusted iron that ran around the middle. You could see it still had that bulging out effect that gave it four distinct sides, just like the handheld version, though these were thick ridges of material designed to reinforce the entire structure as well. The ridges ran vertically down the entire length of the bell, ending at the bottom in heavy loops that must have been for some kind of supports. The wooden bell form was a good nine feet wide, at least, and at a guess, eight feet tall. It had been oiled and polished to such a degree that it still shone under the flashlight's beam, albeit dully. Then I realized, as I stepped closer, the dullness wasn't an effect of the polish. No, the wood had absorbed enough oils that it too, just like the fatwoods of the still-living trees in Saltbrook, had petrified during the cold flooded decades. The smoothed wood had taken on the textured polish of marble, and I could see the swirls of grain in the light. Even closer, and I could see what had really dulled the flashlight's beam— carvings running across the entire outside surface of the bell. Shapes and cuneiforms, curves and lines that teased the eye to follow them. So minute in detail that they would've been impossible to notice on the smaller handbell. So pervasive that they were numerous enough to refract and distort the light in all sorts of strange ways.

I righted the overturned worktable and stood up on it. This was a casting form, which means the finished bell would have been the same size, but this was far too big to have been mounted somewhere in the church, which is where I'd first thought they had placed it. I thought maybe if I could get a look at the top of it and see how it was mounted, I could have some idea of where it had been hung. The flashlight played off of a smoothed top, however— just a gracefully curved shallow dome, with gratings carved into it at the four cardinal points. No mounting or hanging point of any kind.

I stepped off the table and looked again at the bottom of the bell. The four loops carved into the main vertical supports, each one a good six inches thick. The gratings at the other end. The commemoration festival as a deadline. The pieces, all of them started coming together, all at once. I knew where Wallace would be, where the final key had to be used, I had almost all of it! I set off turning and leaving the shop and the bell form behind. Once out in the courtyard, I just cheated and ran around the rest of the building to get back to the road, and started running down what remained of the road ahead of me. Rain either began to fall right then, or had started sprinkling just before, but it didn't matter if it was coming down or not. We, and the entire valley, were running out of time.

11. Ring

I had the radio out and was switching it back on before I even cleared the foundry fully because I had to get confirmation of what I was thinking already. "Cas! Cas, are you there?"

"You're back! Good, was starting to get worried, I—"

"No time for that. I think you need to get out of the valley. Like, right now." I was on the road by that point, moving ahead into a full-on run. So far, the rain was only spare droplets but every one of them was big, fat, and ice cold. This was going to be a nasty storm when it finally hit. Thunder rumbled and rolled faintly through the air, and while the darkness was almost total now, it was broken by the occasional flash of cloud-to-cloud lightning.

"Why?" he asked, alarm fighting with caution in his voice.

"The cult. They really did have a bell made, only it — No it's going to take too long to explain. Short version— big bell, and I think they hung it directly under the well, upside down, so it would use the entire valley as an amplifier." The road turned slightly and became a downhill slope. Given the angle, I was guessing it was going to be all downhill from here to the creek bed. At least I hadn't had to come up this way.

"Woah."

"Yeah, only I don't think they counted on the caves underneath—"I ducked under a low-hanging branch. Damnit, the trees were getting in closer too as I went. There'd been some buildings visible facing the street before, but a lot of this part of the town had been cheaper and more lightly constructed— most of it swept away in the flood, and what had been left behind hadn't given the new growth of trees much competition. Which meant the forest had grown in thick and a lot closer to the road. It was rapidly becoming less of a road and more a tree-covered tunnel.

"The karst." Cas corrected me.

"Whatever. I don't think they planned on the karst being there. If the bell's hanging *in* the karst it's going to act like one giant subwoofer, right? Amplify the sound even more?"

"Right up until the vibrations cause everything on top of the karst to collapse. If it's big enough it'd be just like a full-on earthquake. Oh. Fuck. I need to get out of the valley. So do you." I wish. I dodged under another branch, and then jumped over another fallen branch almost right after. I started slowing down some. Full tilt, downhill into an obstacle course was no one's idea of fun.

"Can't. Still have to get Wallace, or at least the keys. Plus, maybe I can stop this from happening."

"So, this is what Wallace was after? Why hasn't he set it off yet?" Cas asked.

"I don't know, but I don't want to risk anyone else being down here when he does. But the keys unlock the bell-strikers, one for each side of the bell. That big log under Town Hall had to be one of them. And then the fifth key must set the whole thing off."

"Jesus. And the rain's going to soften everything up, make a collapse even worse. All right, I'm moving and heading out. Where are you going?"

"The well. See if I can catch Wallace there and stop this before it all happens. I think the fifth key must get used somewhere near it. Then I'm getting the fuck out. If I'm not up at the station by dawn..."

"You'll be up at the Station. I'll see you there. Anything else you need?"

"Knowing I'm not risking anyone other than me is enough for right now. Over and out."

"Good luck. Over and out." I switched the radio fully off and moved it to the back of my belt while I kept moving. If Cas was being good and bugging out, then it'd be useless all too quickly anyway. I was just glad he hadn't had the presence of mind to ask *why* about any of what I'd told him. Aside from the explanation taking too long, I was worried I'd sound like a lunatic. They planned all this? To die, and then have the bell bring them back to life? That sounded like it fit with Theresa's rhetoric. But they hadn't planned on the dams, or the flooding. Not originally. The well and the bell had been set up before that decision had ever been made. So what bodies would they go back into? That kitten may have been alive, but it certainly hadn't looked any healthier than when it had been dead.

The tree tunnel began to widen out as the road began leveling out from the downhill slope, and I emerged back out into the storm again. The rain was staring to come down heavier already, and even as I picked up speed, I was getting quickly soaked. I tried to remember what I could of Cas's map— the road I was on should be a straight shot into the town plaza, but the creek bed should be coming up, and between the darkness and the storm darkening up everything further, I was now down to just what my flashlight could show me for visibility. Under my still-moving feet, I could see a sudden shift— bricks and dirt road giving way to flatly leveled boards, and I came to a halt, bringing the light around.

It was a bridge. The creek bed was wider here, my light just barely reached the far side, a good twenty feet away, and ran just as deep as earlier, if not deeper. The bridge ahead looked like it was still all here, but past the narrow starting piling of concrete I stood on now, most of the rest of the structure was wood— they'd never updated it for heavier traffic before the flooding. A sudden flash of lightning in the distance ahead of me threw the bridge into stark silhouette, momentarily illuminating the skyline of the town beyond. I was so *close*. I didn't have time, the storm was only going to get worse at this point, and trying to cross when it was fully pouring would be even more hazardous if boards started breaking. I backed up a few paces and took it at a full run, flashlight swinging in front of me to light the way.

My boots hit the wood with a dull thud as I went across, most of them shaking with the vibration. By my fifth step, I could swear I'd felt some of them breaking already. By the ninth, I could see the gap up ahead— the final three feet of the bridge's floorboards were gone, broken through already by age or some unwary tourist, but either way, they weren't *there* and I only had a few steps before I hit that gap. Two more steps and on the third, I sunk down and launched myself up and across the gap. Behind me, I could hear wood breaking and pieces falling and bouncing off the rock of the creek bed. No time for watching the damage, though, I hit the ground running and kept going, and the storm picked up the pace with me, finally breaking in full with another crash of lightning and thunder, rain pouring down over me and everything else in thick sheets of water.

I knew I was passing buildings and houses, but I couldn't look up to check— the rain had gotten intense enough that I had to keep my head down, just so I could pull in air that wasn't half-full of water. I slowed for a moment at the first cross street, looking up to see where I was, my boots sliding to a stop across the wet bricks. There was almost a good inch of water collecting in the streets, with so many drainage points filled with dirt and debris, all it could do was pool and start flooding all over again.

Looking up and around, I still had a block to go. I shook my head, feeling the bun that my braid had been in finally coming fully loose between the weight of the water and all the activity I'd gone through— fuck it, I shook my hair fully out of the bun, letting the braids fall back down to full length. At this point things were messed up enough I might as well just let them loose. I started moving forward again, taking it at a slow jog, one hand up and shielding my eyes from the rain, the other holding the flashlight.

The pitch-blackness of the storm and the night somehow made the wide-open plaza feel much more closed in than it actually was. Everything was as quiet and still as I'd left it, save for the water sheeting down across every surface. As I walked towards the north end of the plaza and the well, I corrected myself— not *everything* was as I'd left it. Shining the light around the plaza, I could see someone had picked up Theresa's head from the ground and placed it back onto the rest of her body, where it had been petrified onto the tree, though the extra piece that had fallen off from her forehead was still gone. Another flash of lightning ran across the sky, silhouetting the tree and church against the clouds. From here, the light also caught out what looked to be someone's leg sticking out just a bit from behind the well, and a few scattered objects on the ground around it.

I circled around carefully, keeping my focus on that leg. It was Wallace. Or at least, Wallace's corpse, slumped in a sitting position with his back up against the northeast side of the well. Like before, he didn't appear to be breathing. The far-too-loose suit had developed even more stains and filth since I'd seen him last, and discoloration from fluids starting to settle with gravity showed up as deep red and purple bruise-like marks in his jaw and chin as well as the exposed hands where they drooped on the plaza. The hole I'd left in his shoulder had long since stopped draining out fluids, and at this angle was starting to collect its own separate pool of water. All around him were scattered a number of ancient, rusty, and damaged tools salvaged, at a guess, from the nearby buildings. Also, my light played across one other object near the edge of the scattered group of items— *my gun.* I kept the light and my eyes on Wallace, and slowly crouched down to pick it up.

The metal barrel made a scrape against the bricks as I wrapped my hand around the grips of the gun, and in response, a gurgling wheeze came from Wallace's body as it pulled in air, and I nearly jumped out of my skin despite having both eyes fully on the bastard and waiting for it to happen. Not-Wallace slowly opened one eye, then the other, a weird, disjointed movement that somehow made the act seem utterly alien, though both eyes now being completely filmed-over like cataracts from decomposition certainly didn't help.

"Detective." Not-Wallace's voice had become even more liquid-filled and burbling than his breathing. "So good of you to" a pause as he wheezed in another breath "join us. Almost thought you weren't coming." Another pause. "I'd get up, but Wallace's legs stopped working sometime yesterday. I think his spine finally gave out."

"Good, it means I won't have to shoot you more. And of course I came back. I still need those keys. I think I'm filing you away as 'unrecoverable', on the other hand."

He laughed in response, more of a gross burbling sound than anything else, but I managed to get the gist of it, then inhaled another big wet breath. "And did you see what I wanted you to? Do you understand why I had to do this?"

I squatted down. Not that I wanted to get on his level particularly, but it gave me a better angle to look for the keyring, which I still wasn't seeing, and to stretch my legs from a different position. Just about everything was sore at this point. I needed to keep him talking, maybe he'd give up a hint on where the keys were. "I saw a lot of things. Some of them didn't quite make sense. How about you put them all together for me, since you're in a talking mood?"

There was another wet noise that may have been a cough or a bark of a laugh. "Fair enough, detective. But I did not spend all this time following the keys out of this valley and bringing them back for nothing. We'll have a little fun with this. You tell me who I am, and I'll give you everything you wanted to know."

My mind was racing. *Followed the keys.* "I knew you were one of the ghosts from the town, possessing that body." I began. "But you're not Thomas, which is what I thought at first, since he was the one who took the keys out of the valley before it flooded fully, right?"

"Right so far, Detective. Very astute."

"And you didn't know where the key mechanisms were. Not exactly. The only reason you had to be in the church was to look for one, and you didn't know where it was. You don't give a shit about the cult, or you would have had more respect for the body under Town Hall. You didn't die in the flood, you died before the flood ever happened. But you knew the bell and the keys existed. You knew they existed, but they never let you get your hands on the keys after you finished the bell, did they, Dubrovsky?"

He made a noise not unlike a cat hacking up a hairball at the mention of his name, began laughing, and after a moment spat out a wet mass of what looked like esophageal tissue, blackened blood, and still—moving insect larvae onto the ground, all while continuing that terrible laugh. "*Very* good, Detective. Well done. Yes. Very well done indeed. You've earned your questions. Ask."

"All right. Why? Why all of this, why try to set the bell off now after all this time?"

"Would have done it sooner, but this was the first time someone had moved or touched the keys in years."

"You could only take someone over if they were holding the keys?"

"Yes. Death works differently for everyone. Things that are simple rules for some don't exist for others. I needed to see those keys work, so I was able to hang on to them after death. But now? I'm trapped in what's left of this body. Cannot even finish what I started, because too much is wearing away." He held up both hands, and I could see where decaying flesh must have failed time and time again as he worked— Fingers had lost joints and whole bones as ligaments and skin and muscle gave way to hang raggedly, savage chunks had been ripped from the palms where he must have tried to force items to do what he'd needed to turn those keys. "Still," he continued. "Work is almost finished. Soon, it will ring."

"What does the bell do, exactly?" I inquired. "I saw the demonstration with the kitten, but that wasn't exactly bringing it back to life, was it?"

"Again, very good. For Theresa, there was no difference. Her *little*—" I heard a wet pop on the last word and saw one corner of his jaw suddenly hanging lower than the other. He reached up, massaging it back into place with the stumps of his fingers. "Her little miracle, the bitch called it. She believed. But the bell does not bring life. The sound of the bell affects all spirits who hear it, but they are not *made alive*. Death cannot be undone. But the bell strengthens spirits. If body and spirit both are nearby, it becomes easy for any spirit to slip right back in, take it over like nothing happened. Spirit goes back into its own body, it's easy for the little automatic things to come back— heart beats again, lungs move, but the body is still dead."

"Then what happened when she had you use a bell on Augustus?"

"Like I said— spirit came back, but the body was still dead. Church ended up keeping him preserved in bandages to trot out at town meetings. He was little more than a puppet when alive to begin with, so not much changed there."

"And with this bell? What happens to all the spirits here? The bodies are long gone for the most part, and the few left are petrified. What happens when they hear the bell?"

Dubrovsky leaned forward. "See? This is *why*. This is why I am here, and I am thinking it is becoming why you are here as well. I must find out. I must *know*. The original bell was an old magic, from my grandfather's grandfather's time. But always small. Always tiny. No one has ever made such a bell, not so big, not so powerful. Couldn't even test the bell while I was alive, the metal needed ten years at least to settle, to be perfect, before it rang or it would crack. But now? It is ready. It is waiting. And I *must* see what happens."

While Dubrovsky talked, it started getting noticeably lighter. I didn't look up at first, focused instead on him, but as it continued I realized it couldn't be the storm fading— the rain was no less intense, and by now it would've been fully dark anyways. I finally broke off eye contact from Dubrovsky's clouded, rheumy gaze and looked out at the plaza. It was slowly filling. Not just with water, though we were definitely above the two-inch waterline now across the plaza. No, first one, then two, then more and more of the ghosts appeared. No flickering, no shifting, every detail of them visible, as if the sheeting rains acted to somehow stabilize their appearance. All of them, men, women, even the children, casting the same cold ghostly light, filling the plaza with it. They kept coming, filling the square. And then Theresa flickered into existence in front of the group, barely ten feet away from me. None of them moved. None of them spoke. All of them solely focused on us, on *me* with those same mirror-bright eyes.

"You, I think, are coming to share my need as well."

Dubrovsky wheezed. "You too need to see what happens."

It took me a second to break my gaze away from the assembly of the dead. "No. I'm just here to take the keys and go. Finishing the job."

"If you can just walk away from this, then do. You are welcome to it. The keys—" he pointed with the remains of one hand towards the north side of the well "are there. In the mechanism. Though, to my frustration, it refuses to turn. That was what finally stopped me."

I slowly rounded the well, keeping an eye on both Dubrovsky and the ghosts as best I could, though none of them moved. "Is the lock broken?" I asked, half-curious, half-stalling.

"Mechanism is in good order." Dubrovsky replied. "They built to my specifications, and built well. I designed all of this to last through anything." There. I could see them. My first time through here, it had just looked like a small hump of settled lake debris, but Dubrovsky and the rains had cleared it fully away— a small diagonal slab of stone at the base of the well, six inches across, with a rotating lock set into it. And sticking out of the lock was the brass key, still hooked on to the others. I pulled it out of the lock and my own curiosity got the better of me. I turned it over in my hands, looking over the object I'd spent days searching for. It was built similarly to any old key from the previous few centuries— a round oval of a handle, a cylindrical barrel, about four inches long, and four teeth, cast in a symmetrical pattern. Looking at the underside of the barrel, though, I noticed one thing Dubrovsky must have missed— there, just behind the last of the teeth was a small slot, just over a quarter of an inch long and maybe an eighth of an inch thick. I looked up at the assembled ghosts, at Dubrovsky, at Theresa.

"She really never trusted you." I said to him. "It's not the mechanism. It's the key. She took your pattern, but then she changed the lock afterward. The key's missing a tooth." I let my flashlight drop to hang off the lanyard around my wrist, and tucked the gun into the waistband of my pants. It wasn't a burning need to do this. Or any kind of compulsion. I just had to see if my hunch was right. Simple, stupid curiosity. I reached into my pocket, shifted my gaze to the assembly of ghosts in the plaza, and pulled out the necklace. It was still cold to the touch, but when I pulled it out, there was no change in the ghosts filling the plaza. Just a feeling of pressing *need* that grew more and more intense. I turned back to the key. The bottom of the necklace's cross popped into the slot perfectly, and I could feel the weight of the key shift in my hand as some internal mechanism in the barrel shifted down, presumably to lock the new piece into place.

Looking again at the necklace, I could see one horizontal line on the silver, just below where the base met the other parts of the circled cross— not a decoration, but a perforation added by someone with a chisel later on. A quick twist of the hand snapped the metal off on the line, breaking the rest of the jewelry away from the key, and I held up the newly finished brass and silver key, letting what was left of the necklace drop to the ground.

"Ah. So it was." Dubrovsky said. "And now? Will you walk away from all this? Will you let this great question remain unanswered?"

"Fuck yes I will." I started to stand up from where I'd crouched over the lock mechanism, and that was when Theresa seized her moment. I don't know if it was me assembling the key or holding onto it that suddenly gave her a surge of power, or if she'd just been biding her time, but she flickered across the gap between us almost instantly, grabbing my hand that held the key in one ice-cold hand, and my other arm in the other. Her lips moved, but no sound that I could hear issued forth, and with an inexorable strength that defied any attempt I could make to resist her, she forced my hand and arm down, pushing the end of the key into the locking mechanism and turning it. I screamed as something popped in my wrist, but then she let go of my hand and used both of her hands to heave me up and over out of her way, in her rage not even caring about which direction I went as I fell directly into the well.

I heard Dubrovsky yell in protest as I went over the edge. It felt like I was hanging there forever, suspended in air and darkness, though it could have only been seconds, and then I landed, flat on my back, on a cold metal floor, knocking the breath out of me. I doubled over in pain, gasping to recover, and as I did so, realized I could feel everything around me starting to vibrate. I got up to my knees, pulling out my flashlight.

It was, well, about what you'd expect for being inside a giant bell. A cylindrical chamber, the walls and floor of that same mix of bronze with other dark reddish inclusions like the handbell. Rain sheeted down into here, still pouring so quickly it made breathing difficult, through the open mouth of the well above me, and drained slowly away through the grating in the bottom of the bell. My hands touched the wall, tracing the cuneiform markings I'd seen on the outside of the bell. Here on the inside, reversed, to the touch the lines and ridges felt more like shapes— like outstretched limbs, screaming howling faces pushed into the metal. Everything kept shaking with rhythmic vibrations, like the ticking of the clock, I had a moment to realize it had to be the mechanism at work, and then the bell itself moved downwards, slowly lowering on chains that ran up from the loops on the edge of the bell to anchors above, moored in the stone of the well.

The top edge of the bell was only a little over six and a half feet high. I could jump that distance, grab the top, and climb onto the chain, then go up the inside of the well. I had just enough time to plan that far out in my mind, and then the first striker hit the bell.

There was no sound. Not that I could hear. No note, no noise, just an overwhelming crushing force that came in from all sides and lifted me off my feet up into the air as the first striker hit. I felt pain as ribs popped, lungs deflated, bones crushed, and muscle and skin tore, and then I was whole again, and the second striker hit before my feet could even touch the ground. The crushing force of vibrations gripped me again, water thrown up from the walls and floor merging with the rain still falling down making everything feel as if the bell was filled with water, as if I was floating, freezing, and drowning, and just as suddenly not. And then another striker hit, pain burning and searing through me, and another, and the first one coming back from the first swing to strike again, and over and over just... floating there, in the void. Feeling the water in the air all around me, lungs burning to hold onto what breath I could, eyes shut tight because for some reason I couldn't dare to look, as if looking would somehow make it all the more real. My outstretched hands reach blindly, hoping to find which way was even upwards, and touched metal that was even colder than the water surrounding me, metal so cold it burned and vibrated as the striker shit again in a renewed set of reverberations, ringing out a tune that no one could hear, but I could feel with every last nerve and cell of my body and...

It went on for hours. It went on for only a moment. It went on forever. Pain and agony and death and rebirth and life again and again and again, with the crushing force of those vibration waves hammering through every inch of me with each strike. Over and over. Until everything was darkness and silence.

12. Wake

I came back into consciousness just as suddenly as I'd been knocked out of it, gasping for breath as I lay in a crouch on the bottom of the bell, the metal still quivering in the aftermath. From some distance away, above me but not far enough above to be above the ground, I could hear the sound of things crashing and falling away— at a guess, parts of the mechanism anchored to structures that wouldn't have survived. I searched across the floor, my hands finally encountering the barrel of my flashlight, and I picked it up, hitting the switch at the same time, only to be rewarded with the tinkling sound of broken glass landing on metal. At a guess, both the bulb and the supposedly shatterproof glass of the lens had been crushed in everything. I'd have to make do with what I remembered, and what I could see in the faint ghostlight still coming in through the top of the well, which wasn't much.

The top of the bell wouldn't have changed position, though, so I gathered myself up and surged up into a jump, hands and arms extended to grab onto the edge as I came into contact with it. There was a moment of freefall in that darkness that made me think I'd made a mistake, or maybe the outer wall of the bell was gone or some other horrible thing, and then my palms solidly caught metal with a jarring impact I felt down into my shoulders. My right wrist screamed internally in protest where Teresa had hurt it before, but I kept my grip and pulled myself up until I could get my waist above the level of the bell. At about two inches thick it wasn't comfortable by any stretch, but I was able to brace my weight there and shift a hand over to the nearest chain on my right for a better grip while I levered one leg up onto the edge. From there it was a slow balancing act, getting my other leg brought up so I could stand on the bell's edge while bracing myself with one hand on the chain and the other stretched up to brace on the inside of the well.

And of course, it was there, standing on a two-inch wide edge of a bell that swung freely, upside down, in a three-foot gap below the bottom of a fake well, over a karst of unknown size and depth, that I felt the sudden lurch and shift of one of the chains starting to give way on the other side of the bell. Holding onto the chain with one hand, I grabbed out my knife with the other, unfolding it one-handed and reaching up as far as I could, trying to feel for a break in the mortar between the stones of the well. While the well's exterior had been worn smooth with turbulence and currents over the years of the flood, the interior stayed mostly preserved— using natural stones mortared together made the inside walls almost a perfect climbing wall, if I could get far enough up it to brace myself before the bell fell away and if the mortar held strongly enough.

The blade slipped on the first attempt, and I had to juggle keeping a grip on the knife and keeping balance on the bell simultaneously, but then on a second, frantic swing, the knife held, sinking in a good two inches between the stones at almost the limit of my reach. I held on and pulled myself upward, boots seeking purchase on the lower edge of rocks for a moment before I managed to gain purchase. I heard a tortured shriek of metal below me, and reflexively looked down, as yet another bolt of lightning slammed across the sky. Illuminated briefly in the flash, I could see the bell, chains broken and falling away, already a good fifty feet below me, and even further below that, at least a hundred feet down, the white limestone floor of the karst reflected back the light, showing scattered debris and pieces of bronze and wood clockwork already littering it. Fuck. If the mechanism was collapsing that quickly, more was sure to be following it soon, and so help me, I wasn't going to join the pile. I started climbing as quickly as I could on the wet rocks.

The climb itself only took a few minutes, though it felt far longer as I strained up for handhold after handhold. But I did notice one thing as I climbed, and when I got out to the surface, my attention was focused completely on that at first— I wasn't hurt. Anywhere. Aside from a sore line across the bottom of my ribs that might have been a bruise from the edge of the bell, every injury, every bruise and scrape I'd taken before going into the bell was gone as if it had never happened. That was eerie enough on its own, but as I looked around, I realized there was even more strangeness going on in the wake of the bell's sounding.

The ghosts were gone. Wallace's remains were still slumped at the base of the well, but there was no sign of any of the town's inhabitants. Instead, the entire plaza, and what I could see of the town beyond it, now glowed with the ghostly light that had been shed by the spirits themselves, like some kind of background radiation. It ran through everything, making no difference between brick, wood, or stone, even the trees glowed with the same pale radiance. It was dimmer, though, patchy, like it had been stretched and strained out to cover all this surface until it was full of holes and gaps. It gave me just enough light to see general shapes by, but that was about it. Moreover, the light moved — it roiled and shifted all on its own, coiling through the structures like a living thing. It almost reminded me of the hangman's tree, the way it moved.

"This is *not* the acid trip I asked for." After everything else, I wasn't about to hold back the commentary now. I was more surprised, though, when Wallace's mouth opened up and Dubrovsky let out a bitter laugh in response.

"You're still here?" I asked.

"Surprisingly, yes," he replied. "Though I can feel myself beginning to fade now. Though the same could be said of you. You survived something that should have killed you a dozen times over." As he spoke, I could see that he was telling the truth in at least one way— Wallace's body, already so damaged and decayed, was beginning to come apart at the seams. Bones had been shattered in the vibrations from the bell— I could see pieces sticking out from wounds on his chest and upper arms. Wallace's skin was also showing the strain— tearing away over the joints, across stretch-points on his throat and cheeks, all over.

"Well, whatever happened down there, it didn't kill

me. I'm still here." And how sure of that was I? No, no time to think about it now. "So, where did everyone go?"

"Go?"

"Yes. The other ghosts. Theresa. Where'd they all go?"

"I don't think you understand, Detective. The bell worked just as I thought it would. The ghosts were revitalized by the sound, and went into the nearest available bodies." Thunder crashed again, this time further away to the west, but I still found myself yelling over it.

"But there aren't any available bodies! Everything human is—" I broke off as the realization hit me. "No one said they had to be human bodies."

"Indeed."

"They're in the town."

"They *are* the town, Detective. And, I think, stretched far enough out to be in the Valley as well. They're just starting to wake up in there, figuring out what they can do. Well, most of them." Before I could say anything else, I heard a sharp crack and pop of stone breaking against stone followed by the clunk of heavy chain falling onto the bricks of the plaza behind me. I had enough presence of mind to think about how much of an idiot I'd been to put my back towards the church while I'd been talking to Dubrovsky while I spun around to face what was coming next, and then Theresa was nearly on me.

She was in her own body at least, though that also made this all the more horrific at the same time — petrified flesh and bone cracked at each joint as she moved them, the pieces holding together and defying gravity through what seemed to be pure force of will alone. Her first steps were lurching but she rapidly picked up speed, coming at me with both arms outstretched, fingers curled into claws, mouth still open in a scream-like rictus.

I acted on pure reflex, grabbing the Glock out of the shoulder rig and firing four shots right into her torso, splintering out chunks of her and she kept coming straight on at me, one swinging arm knocking the pistol flying out of my hand. I raised my arm to block her strike with her other hand, but she simply grabbed my forearm in a crushing grip, and brought the other hand back around, which I grabbed, before she could do anything further. While she might have had the advantage in terms of pure strength, I had weight and density I could use against her. I shifted us into a turn, and she still tried to overpower me and lean in against me, jaw cracking and moving, as she tried to move her jaw to speak, even if there were no lungs or vocal chords to produce a sound any longer. I kicked up and out as hard as I could, feeling a satisfying pop as shoulders pulled free from sockets, and Theresa's body spun back and over the edge of the well. I threw the arm I was holding onto in after her, and the other loosened its grip almost immediately after pulling free of her body. It lay twitching on the ground as I went back to the north side of the well, where Theresa had left the keys inside the mechanism, and pulled them free of the lock, stuffing them back into my pocket, with the bronze key poking up out of it.

"Any more surprises?" I asked Dubrovsky as I walked back around the well. Wallace's corpse had tilted forward during the fight or when Theresa went over the well, and it seemed to sever whatever connection Dubrovsky had left. There was no response. He was finally gone. Good. Time for me to be gone as well. As if to punctuate the thought, I could feel the ground beneath me hitch and rumble, like a small wave had gone through it.

While I traveled a lot, I technically lived in upstate New York. Earthquakes weren't a common thought for me, much less the idea of aftershocks. I hadn't even thought of those as a possibility with the bell, but here we were, the ground beginning to ripple and roll. I took one look back, long enough to see the church start to tilt and sway like a ship at sea before it started to crumble, and then I ran, putting on every last bit of speed I had in me, straight south down the road out of town and towards the ridge. As I ran, the town began to shift — Dubrovsky had been right about the spirits now stuck in the materials of the town itself just waking up because that was exactly what was starting to happen. Walls shifted, extending into twisted faces and hands, some normally sized, others distended, twisted, huge constructs. I saw one building ahead of me suddenly extend out huge arms of bricks and wood that pushed out and down as if it was trying to push itself up off the ground, and then the walls, suddenly lacking the material support they needed, collapsed in on themselves. A gaping mouth, six feet across, opened up in the road ahead of me, teeth and lips all formed out of whole and broken bricks. I jumped over it, looking down for a moment at an open throat that went clear down into the caves below, landed hard on the other side, rolling and sliding back up into a run as the mouth collapsed in on itself and fell away.

The worst were the faces— they kept forming and reforming, following me along the walls as I went. A few would stare impassively at me, but most were twists of rage and frustration, the slick of rainwater almost making them look as if they were crying, angered at having been awoken and freed from their ghostly loops of memory, only to be fully physically trapped within the town itself as it now collapsed. I risked a look over my shoulder— the ripples were still coming, spreading out further and wider, but behind me, I could see the church, the well, and most of the plaza gone already, crumbled and fallen down into the ever-widening pit that was the center of town. The ground under me began to shift and roll again as the waves caught up to me, and I tripped and stumbled as one caught me right when I was ducking under a pair of outstretched hands of stone, nearly falling headlong into another open pit of a mouth. I caught myself in time, sidestepping and ducking one way then another, dodging the new—formed limbs before they could get a grip.

And then I came up to the one thing I'd forgotten about— the root tunnel. Above me to the right, I could see the graffiti of the self-disemboweling rabbit rippling and moving in the ghostlight, the vivid yellow and black eye rolling to watch me as the feet kicked feebly at its own entrails. Ahead was the broken wall that hung over the tunnel itself, the entrance from this side choked thickly with plant roots and vines. And looking behind me, there was no way I was going to have time to double back or go around, the edge of the hole the town was falling into was now a block and a half away at most, and spreading. I aimed for the low side of the overhang to the right and jumped, pulling myself up on the cracked edge of the wall. Up here, it was almost like running through the forest again— fresh growth of trees and moss carpeted almost the entire surface, leaving only a few bare patches of wet concrete as I ran.

And of course, it was when I was up there that the next wave of aftershocks caught up to me. The entire slab of wall shifted, and my next step on what I thought was solid mossy ground proved it to be anything but, as I plunged down into the tunnel, fibrous tendrils of roots clutching at me as I fell. I landed hard, the shock shooting pain up through both ankles into my legs, my hands catching and scraping on sharp concrete edges. I was in the dark again, barely able to breathe from all the tightly pressed in plant matter, and I could feel the shake of the earth still moving. I fought down a rising wave of panic and blindly pushed forward. I had to assume I fell still pointed towards the exit. I'd been at least halfway across. I didn't have far to go. I had to move. And so I did. I fought against the pain and the grabbing roots and dragged myself forward, slogging through the mass. Holding my breath except for quick gasps of air. Five steps. Ten. I could see flickers of ghostlight, illuminating the forest ahead. Fifteen, I was almost in the clear, just reaching the last stage of the tunnel that was mostly plant-free. Which is when the spirits stuck in the plants of the tunnel took their moment to seek out revenge, thick wet bundles of roots behind me suddenly whipped forward, wrapping themselves around my wrists and my neck, strangling me and lifting me off my feet. I gasped for air, fighting to get to my knife, to get to anything to get the roots off me. The plants started glowing, brighter and brighter as they tightened their grip on me, but my vision began to shrink down to a pinpoint, blacking out as I was being choked out.

Behind me, I could hear the rumble of another aftershock getting close, and the tunnel around me started to fill with dust as the slab overhead started to fully give way and collapse. The roots holding me suddenly slumped and dropped me to the ground, falling apart as they broke off from the plants they were connected to. I fell limply to the ground and rolled forward without meaning to, carried into a somersault that ended with me flat on my stomach, just feet away from being out the tunnel. Above me, the concrete pitched and broke, the slab slowly starting to come down. I didn't have the strength left to pick myself up. I could barely breathe, barely even see or think. I dragged myself forward on my arms, crawling slowly and steadily. When the slab fell, dropping around me in pieces, burying me in loose soil and dirt, I felt the wave of darkness and loss of consciousness swell and rise up into me at the same time.

I came to moments or hours later, I don't know how long it had been. Still covered in piles of earth rapidly turning into mud in the rain that was finally beginning to slow, though I could breathe. Something heavy was pinning my left foot right around the heel. I twisted around and sat up, looking behind me. The tunnel was gone, the slab and everything on it fallen to pieces in a massive pile of debris, half of which was now down in the pit that had stopped expanding for the moment. But my heel was stuck under the very corner of a ten-foot wide thick slab of wall that had managed to remain intact. Shooting pain pinched through that heel as the slab settled a little further, increasing the pressure on it. I tugged weakly with my leg, then got both hands shifted through the earth to grab just below my knee. It wasn't coming free, and I had no way to shift that slab. Worse, I could already feel the shifting rumble of yet another aftershock. That pit was going to start expanding again in a moment. It was a desperate effort, but I reached down, scrabbling with aching fingers to reach my bootlaces. A few quick pulls and I had the knot out and the upper part of the boot loosened. One tugging kick, then another, and I managed to extract my foot, still in what was left of the sock. It hurt like hell, but I got myself upright, limping free of the wreckage of the overhang.

I was out of the town but still had the road through the woods ahead of me. Out here, the ghostlight was sparser, infecting individual trees seemingly at random most of them far enough away that I wasn't worried about an animated tree suddenly coming after me. I staggered forward as fast as I could, pain shooting up from my heel with every step. I didn't have any sense of time or distance left, there was only the agonizing lurch forward. I was following the trail more by feel than any actual light or sound, aside form the continued flashes of lightning, though those had grown far more sparse. Behind me, though, I could hear rumbling. The pit didn't seem to be expanding at this point, just everything that had fallen in shifting with the latest wave of shakes. I kept limping forwards, over hardpacked wet ground. Ahead of me, I could see the silhouette of the empty Victorian house I'd passed on my way in, an empty black shape against a sky that was starting to show patchy spots of open stars. As I went past the front, I could hear movement, from that open hole into the basement where I'd discovered the camper's skeleton. I did not look in. I didn't want to add another horror to the pile collecting in my mind. My heel was beginning to go numb from wet, cold, and repeated abuse, and I found myself picking up the pace to get away.

More steps. More time numbly passed. I made the distance from the house to the clearing where my campsite had been in a daze. Cas had been good to his word, though, he was gone, with no trace of my own camp left behind. The clouds were gone, the moon set, the stars giving enough light to see by, though I was betting I'd see the lightening on the eastern horizon soon for dawn. Part of me wanted to sit, but I needed to get the fuck out. I pressed on. It was when I got past the campsite and back into the tree-lined roadway that I heard another big crackling rumble from the center of the valley. This was a big one. Everything pitched and shook around me, and even with the injuries, I found myself running again, fast as I could still manage. Ahead of me, I could see trees suddenly pitch over and fall, or worse, ones that simply dropped straight down. This was it— the rest of the valley was going to go. I put my head down and pushed even harder. I don't know when I made it past the empty hole of a foundation that had been my first view of the ruins in the valley, but I remember seeing huge cracks in the ground in every clearing I passed, plants and earth tumbling away into the karst below.

When I hit the hill that was the base of the ridgeline, I started climbing, without even bothering to look for the path, hand over hand scrambling up the rocky slope. I was about fifty feet up, halfway up the ridge when the shaking reached its peak, and there in the dim, predawn light I looked out across the valley. Most of it was gone, dropped a good hundred feet or more in a tumble of trees, earth, and wreckage, and the southern edge, the side closest to me, was still crumbling in. As I watched, the entire northwest ridgeline, no doubt still shaking from the repeated aftershocks, began to crumble into the valley in a single massive landslide, dirt and rocks tumbling down over everything that had fallen into the pit. I hung there for long minutes, catching my breath, watching the dust settle.

I had somehow, despite everything, survived.

Epilogue

The remainder of the climb out had been far easier, without the rest of the valley shaking. The landslide from the northwestern ridge seemed to have been the final cap on all the destruction. I remember limping my way past the remains of Wallace's car, and nearly falling over when Charlie and Cas ran out of the forestry station to meet me. After that had been the longest hottest shower I could manage with the facilities they had, bandaging up my hands and heel, and a long nap on one of their cots. A nap, that thankfully was plagued by no dreams or nightmares whatsoever.

After waking again, and eating and getting my gear together, I bid them both goodbye. They (and I) agreed it'd be best if I was fully gone before anyone arrived on the scene. While the quaking had stayed fairly localized to the valley, there'd still be a slew of questions to answer, especially if extra people like me happened to be around for it. I slipped back into the Suburban and drove off in the early afternoon, texting a quick note to Hollowell about the success of the hunt.

It was early evening when he called me back, just

as I was finishing with filling up my gas tank somewhere near the Washington and Idaho border. I hung up the pump nozzle as I answered the phone. "Lake Services."

"Ms. Lake."

"Hollowell."

"I'm pleased to hear you successfully completed the job. When should I be expecting to see you return with Wallace and the recovered items?" He sounded smug. I wondered, again, about just how much Hollowell actually knew about the valley and its inhabitants.

"Wallace was unrecoverable by the time I caught up to him. My condolences, but your employee is dead. Unfortunately, the body's in a location where the authorities won't be finding him any time soon to confirm that, but we both knew that was a possibility when you contracted me. Your keys, on the other hand, are on their way to you already. I sent them by express mail this afternoon. Inside the package you'll find an account number. I expect a wire transfer for the remainder of my fees, including the full hazard pay, to be paid as soon as possible. My office will send you a digital itemized receipt by email in a few hours, once I've had time to get a hotel room for the night." I turned and went inside the attached convenience store.

"We won't be seeing you in person? That's a shame, Ms. Lake, I'd hoped we might do a debrief of the investigation, just to get something down for our own records. I also had a number of other jobs that I thought you might well be interested in, once you're ready to go out again." I grabbed a pair of bottles of water in my bandaged hand, and some snacks in the other. Road food was always important.

"I'm afraid that won't be possible, Mister Hollowell. I'm going to be unavailable for some time." I turned and went to the cash register to pay.

"Are you sure? I also wanted to make sure you weren't undergoing any lasting side effects from anything that may have happened—"

I cut Hollowell off, hands mechanically going through my wallet and handing the clerk my debit card as I deliberately stared straight at her, giving no attention to the ghost standing in the space just behind her. The spirit there had that same colorless look and mirror bright eyes, aside from that and the fact that the uniform vest he was wearing were straight out of the eighties, the only thing that would have tipped me was the massive shotgun-blast hole that had taken away the upper left half of his head and some of his face. Black blood and other fluids dripped upwards from the hole, evaporating away into thin air.

"No. No side effects, or anything else. Just a normal retrieval job, and some minor scrapes. Otherwise, I'm fine. Now, I need to be driving. I'll email you with anything further." Fully paid, I walked out, still careful to make no eye contact with the ghost. He was the third I'd seen now, and the first one had tried to run up and scream at me when it had realized I could see it.

"Certainly. Thank you again for your quick and thorough services. Goodbye." I got back in the car and started driving. The Ravenswood Institute, whatever it was, was clear across the country. I had a ways to go and a lot of research to do. I wanted to know everything about what shit Hollowell and his people were up to before I got back into their reach again.

DEEARBACAUSKAS

Postscript

Hollowell replaced the ivory-gripped phone receiver back into the brass cradle with a gentle click. It was done. One way or another, even if she had rejected the current offer, the detective would surely be coming round again. It was a shame about Wallace, but then, the man's work had gotten sloppy of late, even before this final incident. He reached out with one hand and closed the main file folder for Saltbrook that he'd left open on the desk, placing it in the tray to be filed in the archives with a number of other items. Underneath was something far more mundane— today's mail. The Institute received so little these days. Two bills, an advertisement from the nearby shopping center, and something else that caught Hollowell's attention. A plain envelope, with the Institute's address typewritten on the front, with a postage paid marker from... 1961. He lit a cigarette, grinding out the match head into the ashtray on his desk, and blew out a thin stream of smoke. He hadn't seen one of these in a few years.

Hollowell picked up and tapped the envelope carefully on the rosewood surface of his desk. This was an old project— one of Tillingher's. Yes. The old Dead Letter Experiment. He'd nearly run out the funding for the postal and secretarial department for five years straight with this one. Thousands of self-addressed pre-paid envelopes, each with a single sheet of paper inside, sent to addresses picked at random from all over the map. Using the postal service as a system of divination. True, it had meant the Institute had been sent back all manner of strange things from assorted newspaper clippings, random letters from people looking for pen pals, and other strange responses. One particularly crafty person had even used it to ship an old console television he'd wanted to get rid of, since the postal service would simply charge the Institute for the extra weight and fees. Hollowell remembered the fight with Tillingher about that one quite well. Still, the system continued to produce the occasional truly interesting result over the years, even after the project had been closed down in 1963. People still occasionally found the envelopes and sent them, and since the account was still paid up, the postal service still delivered.

He finally grabbed out his letter opener and sliced the envelope cleanly at one end, shaking the contents out onto the table. Inside was only the single sheet of paper the Institute had sent out. Unfolding it, Hollowell caught a faint scent off the page. Lilacs and vanilla. Perfume, though definitely not something modern, and a faint whiff under that of something else. Something fouler and more rotten. Someone had taken the time to send a message after all— there was a single word typed across the center of the page, capital letters spaced out to take up even more space.

L E G I O N

Hollowell sat there. Contemplating the page and the word for the remainder of the workday. The cigarette, perched on the edge of the astray, burned itself down to the butt, unsmoked beyond that first drag he'd taken. It was night outside when Hollowell finally shook himself from his reverie, took up his coat and hat, and left the Institute for the evening. If the letter was right, there were not one, but many long and restless nights soon to come.

Saltbrook Area Timeline

1863: Town first founded by initial settlers, including the Morgan family, with a goal of timber harvesting and possible mining.

1864: After several slow deaths, discovery of heavy-metal poisoning from the brook that the town gets it's name from and the main water supply for the town. Three months of continued issues, until the first main well was completed into the clean-running aquifer below the valley.

1865-1900: Slow expansion. Saltbrook never has a full-blown population or work boom due to it's remoteness, but does manage to survive well enough on timber production to remain viable.

1898: Reverend Thomas Fowler and roughly a dozen other members of the Church of Renewed Light, opening the first main church in the town, directly across from Town Hall. The Morgan family among others are the first to convert.

1913: Saltbrook's 50-year commemoration festival, which includes the unveiling of the commemorative well in the middle of the town plaza.

1914-1918: World War 1, and a sudden decrease in town population between the draft and the Church urging all those eligible to serve to do so.

1919: With the death of Thomas Fowler, his grand-niece Theresa Morgan-Fowler assumes control of the Church. With her husband, Augustus serving as mayor. Again, more people continue to leave Saltbrook, as church membership becomes almost mandatory for citizens.

1923: The Coulee Dam survey project begins.

1925: Saltbrook is identified as one of the potential reserve flood locations that feeds into the dam.

1931: After numerous arguments with the Church and town, the State declares Saltbrook valley as a wildlife reserve. Funds are allocated for the relocation of all town members and construction of the blockade dam at the south end of the valley begins, while other rivers and creeks are diverted towards the valley's northern entrance and dammed off. The town is given a three-year deadline to relocate.

1932: The majority of the town relocates to other towns and cities across the state. Of roughly four hundred inhabitants, less than a hundred remain, almost all of them die-hard Church members, believing the town's location chosen for them by God Himself, and intending to stay until the absolute end in 1934 when the planned reservoirs will be directed in to flood the valley.

1933: The Saltbrook Tragedy- flash flooding due to abnormally heavy rains, and either a structural weakness or deliberate sabotage in the northern reservoir dam cause the dam to burst, filling the valley a year early in a matter of three hours. While every attempt is made to evacuate the town, with only one operational main road leading out of the valley thanks to the other two washing out in the rainfall, few survive. Over 85 men, women, and children are unaccounted for and presumed to have perished in the sudden flooding.

1933-1993: Saltbrook Lake remains as a remote body of water and protected wildlife reserve. Visitor demand remains small, and only one beach and a small dock are established for tourists to the area.

1995: Due to other feeder streams and rivers to the Columbia drying up, and with the dam itself fully finished and cured, the decision is made to allow Saltbrook to drain into the main river as originally planned. Demolitions occur in early spring, leaving the entire valley drained to open air for the first time in 62 years.

1996: Two state-funded expeditions into the valley, the first for research and cataloging, the second to find and rescue the first party both disappear into the valley with no apparent survivors. Saltbrook Valley is declared off-limits to the public, and a ranger station is erected at the only entrance left into the valley from public roads.

About The Author

Denice (Dee) Arbacauskas

Dee has most currently been sighted in the Pacific Northwest where she is reported to live. while the Institute does not know her specific whereabouts or activities, it is known that her talents and history include leatherworking, maskmaking, theatre, tattooing, other art forms, parenting, and apparently attempting to survive late-stage capitalism. More info may be obtained at the files located on http://tormentedartifacts.com

Made in the USA
Columbia, SC
14 October 2024

43555794R00130